I can't ~~believe~~
MY MOTHER SAID THAT!

The blood rushed into Julep's head so fast her ears started to ring. Even so, the shrill noise pounding her skull could not drown out the women's giggles. How could her mother have said such a thing? Julep was never going to forgive her. Never! And she was certainly not going out there to face the two of them so they could keep laughing at her.

As she glanced around, Julep felt her breath quicken. She began to panic as the realization hit her: She was trapped in the Limited Too dressing room with no way out.

Okay. Okay. This is not a problem. You will just live here for the rest of your life.

Sure. Live here. Makes perfect sense. You'll order out for pizza. A lot of pizza.

Was she out of her mind? Of course, Julep would have to leave, and when she did, Suzanne and her mother would be waiting to embarrass her again.

Julep's scalp started to itch, and her humiliation began morphing into outright anger. She was tired of her mom taking pleasure in humiliating her. Julep wasn't a little girl anymore. Why, she was nearly a teenager, and it was time to stand up for herself.

Books by Trudi Trueit

Julep O'Toole: Confessions of a Middle Child

Julep O'Toole: Miss Independent

Julep O'Toole: All I Want to Do Is Direct

Julep O'Toole

Miss Independent

Trudi Trueit

PUFFIN BOOKS

PUFFIN BOOKS

Published by the Penguin Group

Penguin Young Readers Group, 345 Hudson Street, New York, New York 10014, U.S.A.

Penguin Group (Canada), 90 Eglinton Avenue East, Suite 700,
Toronto, Ontario, Canada M4P 2Y3 (a division of Pearson Penguin Canada Inc.)

Penguin Books Ltd, 80 Strand, London WC2R 0RL, England

Penguin Ireland, 25 St Stephen's Green, Dublin 2, Ireland
(a division of Penguin Books Ltd)

Penguin Group (Australia), 250 Camberwell Road, Camberwell, Victoria 3124, Australia
(a division of Pearson Australia Group Pty Ltd)

Penguin Books India Pvt Ltd, 11 Community Centre,
Panchsheel Park, New Delhi - 110 017, India

Penguin Group (NZ), 67 Apollo Drive, Mairangi Bay, Auckland 1311, New Zealand
(a division of Pearson New Zealand Ltd)

Penguin Books (South Africa) (Pty) Ltd, 24 Sturdee Avenue,
Rosebank, Johannesburg 2196, South Africa

Registered Offices: Penguin Books Ltd, 80 Strand, London WC2R 0RL, England

First published in the United States of America by Dutton Children's Books,
a division of Penguin Young Readers Group, 2006

Published by Puffin Books, a division of Penguin Young Readers Group, 2007

1 3 5 7 9 10 8 6 4 2

THE LIBRARY OF CONGRESS HAS CATALOGED
THE DUTTON CHILDREN'S BOOKS EDITION AS FOLLOWS:

Trueit, Trudi Strain.

Julep O'Toole : Miss Independent / Trudi Strain Trueit.—1st ed.

p. cm.

Summary: Eleven-year-old Julep O'Toole wants to convince her mom that she is old
enough to wear makeup, have a cell phone, and choose her own clothes, but it takes a
creative idea from the preteen to put mother and daughter on the same wavelength.

ISBN: 0-525-47637-7 (hardcover)

[1. Mothers and daughters—Fiction. 2. Friendship—Fiction.
3. Schools—Fiction. 4. Diaries—Fiction.] I. Title.

PZ7.T78124 Jul 2006

[Fic]—dc22   2005015052

Puffin Books ISBN 978-0-14-240829-2

Printed in the United States of America

For Tucker and her mom, and all the incredible
adventures yet to be

Contents

1 Hot Girl vs. Steamed Mom

Where on Earth did you get *that*?"

The brass-heart key ring slipped from Allison Gallardo-O'Toole's fingertips. Her keys hit the sandy-beige carpet with a *thplud*.

"This?" Julep glanced down at the plum shirt, where a swirl of gold barrel beads splashed the words HOT GIRL across the front. "It's an S.E. tee, Mom."

"A what-ee?"

Zipping her backpack, Julep shouted up the stairs, "Cooper! Let's go."

If her seven-year-old brother didn't get moving, they were not going to get to the corner of Bayview and Chenault on time. Last time they were late, her co-best friend Trig had found a rusty pair of hedge clippers and was turning the Ramplings' boxwood hedge into a French poodle. You never wanted to leave Trig Maxwell and his devious mind alone for more than eight minutes. Julep and her other co-best friend, Bernadette Reed, had timed him. Eight minutes was his limit. After that, there was no telling what he'd do.

It was clear Julep's mother was waiting for a more detailed explanation from her eleven-year-old daughter.

"It's a self-expression tee," said Julep. You had to be from another galaxy not to know about the latest fad. "They say things like SWEET STUFF and BRATTY TO THE MAX. Everybody is wearing them."

"You are not everybody."

Julep snorted. "I knew you were going to say that."

"Then you also know I am going to say there is no way you're wearing *that* to school."

Flipping a springy lock of reddish-brown hair behind one ear, Julep let out a frazzled sigh. No, she hadn't known that. When Julep had convinced her aunt Ivy to buy the shirt for her, she'd had a feeling her mother wasn't going to be thrilled about it. But Julep had not expected a complete parental meltdown. They were just words; two harmless, glittery, swishy words. What was the big problem-o?

Lately, her mother seemed to exaggerate every tiny thing Julep did. The other day, she'd grumbled for most of the evening after Julep had come home from Trig's house a few minutes late. The way her mother had laid into her you'd have thought Julep had been eleven days overdue instead of a measly eleven minutes. Then, yesterday, her mom had burst a few thousand blood vessels because Julep had forgotten to empty the dishwasher. It wasn't like she'd done it on purpose. She'd simply lost track of time turning Bernadette's foot into a rainbow. That's where you paint each toenail a different color of the rainbow. You know, the big toe gets red, the toe next to it is done in orange, and so on down the line with green, blue, and finally violet for the baby toe. In a real rainbow, yellow would be between orange and green, but then a person would have to have six toes like Calvin Kapinski (or so he claimed). Because one color in the foot rainbow has to go, everybody skips yellow because, well, yellow toenails?

Ew. Fungus among us.

Anyway, her mom had stripped Julep of her phone privileges for a whole week because she hadn't gotten her chores done on time. It was S.N.F. (so not fair).

Julep figured her mother's stressful job was partly to blame for her weird behavior. Allison Gallardo-O'Toole was the director of public relations at the Seattle Art Museum. She was in charge of all of the museum's publicity and special events. Whenever anything went wrong, her mother had to swoop in to do what she called "damage control." That meant reassuring the media and the public that everything was under control, even if, sometimes, it wasn't.

Tightening the laces of her tennis shoes, Julep told herself that once the Venetian-glass exhibit ended and people weren't milling too close to priceless, breakable art, her mom wouldn't be quite so touchy. At least, she hoped so. Julep didn't know how much longer she could stand her mother's uptight, easily freakable attitude.

"Julep, did you hear me?"

How could I not? She bit the words in half on her tongue before they could fly out of her mouth.

"Answer me, please. Where did you get that?"

She wished her mother would quit saying the word *that* as if Julep was sporting a dead possum on her chest. Straightening, Julep felt a tingle zip across the top of her skull. An itchy scalp was a sure sign she was starting to get angry.

Take it easy. Just get out the door without getting into another argument.

Julep ran her fingers through the front of her hair, pulling her thick wave of terra-cotta bangs straight up into the air. There was no sense prolonging it. Her mom was going to keep pestering her until she confessed.

"Aunt Ivy," she said.

Her mother slapped her palms together. "I knew it."

Then why did you ask?

"It's no big deal, Mom." Julep madly scratched her right temple. "Bernadette's mom just got her one that says SPOILED ROTTEN."

"Well, that certainly fits."

"It's a little big for her, actually," said Julep, missing her mother's point.

"What that girl needs isn't any more junk. What she really needs is someone to—" Julep's mom stopped when she looked into her daughter's questioning, amber eyes. "Never mind," she said quietly, bending to pick up her car keys off the floor. "I have a meeting to get to. I don't have time for this."

"And I do?" mumbled Julep.

"What did you say?"

"Nothing."

Julep's mom rubbed her forehead with the thumb and index finger of her right hand, a signal that her middle child was starting to give her a headache. "I don't know about your attitude lately, young lady."

My attitude? MY attitude? You are totally kidding me, right?

However, Julep did not dare utter a word. Some things you were not supposed to say because adults didn't want to hear the truth. They were what Julep called the taboo topics and had to be saved for her journal. Thank goodness for her journal! It was the one place where she could write what she was forbidden to utter out loud. Without it, Julep was certain she would have wilted faster than Mrs. Knudsen's Joseph's Coat roses. So many times Julep felt exactly like those flowers: curious and hopeful, but also fragile and temporary. Nobody knew, of course, except her journal. For that was the one place where she was free to be her best and *worst* self—the moody, goofy, lazy, stubborn, unreasonable, S.E.-tee-wearing Julep that wasn't allowed to exist in her mother's world.

Her journal didn't try to change her. It accepted her the way she was. It let her be. Without her journal to confide in, Julep was certain the petals of her spirit would shrivel up and blow away in the wind.

"*That* shirt," her mother said again, "is not appropriate for a girl your age. I'm not even sure if it's appropriate for someone my age."

"They're not meant for old people."

Big mistake. HUGE. She braced for the worst.

Her mother's lips tightened into a white line as she dug through her purse. Much to Julep's surprise, however, she didn't say anything.

This was ridiculous. It wasn't like Julep actually believed she was a HOT GIRL or anything. She wasn't a complete dingleberry. Nobody with eighty-seven freckles sprinkled over her face, a chest flatter than a Fruit Roll-Up, and hair that resembled a tumbleweed in a dust storm could ever be mistaken for a HOT GIRL. Yet that was the whole point of wearing it: to show everyone there was another side to her—a wild, unpredictable side.

If she was lucky, Julep might even get her picture in the What's In? section of the school newspaper. That was where they highlighted the latest catchphrases, fashion trends, music, and crazes going around on campus. Nelson Gibbs, who shot photos for the newspaper and yearbook, always had his digital camera with him in first-period math. Actually, he carried it everywhere. "You have to be ready for any sudden photo op," he'd told Julep when she'd asked him why he lugged so much heavy gear around all the time. "Plus, my dad will kill me if I leave my camera in my locker, and it gets stolen."

"Photo op?" Julep had wondered.

"Opportunity."

Wouldn't it be outrageous if today Julep was Nelson's photo op?

"Julep!" Nelson would call the moment she strolled into math class, his camera flash going off in her face. Before she could blink the spots from her eyes, a herd of photographers would start snapping away.

"Julep, over here," the paparazzi would shout.

"Miss O'Toole, turn this way."

"Julep, your outfit is amazing."

"Thanks." Julep would strike a supermodel runway pose, making sure not to trip over the cord to Mr. Wyatt's overhead projector.

"How does it feel to be voted Best Dressed Girl on Earth?"

"I'm thrilled, of course."

Twirl and pose. Pose and twirl.

"Julep, is it true you're going to Hollywood next week?"

"Well . . . yes. I promised ages ago to style Avril for the Grammys. But that's all I can say." She would raise her hands when pressed for details. "Please, no more pictures. I really must go. Mr. Wyatt is testing us on prime numbers today."

"Just one more pose? It's for the cover of Seventeen."

Well, maybe just one more—for the fans.

"Look this way, Miss O'Toole."

Pop. Pop. Pop. A new shower of flashbulbs would explode.

"Julep, over here."

"Julep!"

"Julep?" Her mother was waving a couple of one-dollar bills at her.

With a depressed sigh, Julep took her lunch money and stuffed it into the front pocket of her jeans. When her mom turned away, she slung her backpack over her shoulder and tip-toed like mad toward the front door. Cooper was on his own now. She was going to make her escape and she was going to do it guilt-free. After all, hadn't Julep almost always followed the rules? Hadn't she almost always done whatever her parents asked of her? So if, for once in her ordinary life, she wanted to wear something extraordinary, was that so horribly wrong? Was that such a crime? Was it too much to ask to let her have this microscopic fleck of joy?

She reached for the doorknob.

"Julep Antoinette O'Toole."

Apparently so.

When your parents use all of your names and dice them like fresh tomatoes, you're shish-kebabed for sure.

Julep dropped her hand first. Then her head. "Yeah?"

"You are not to be seen in *that* at school."

"But, Mooom—"

"Upstairs. Now. Move." Once her mother started barking like the Gunderfests' St. Bernard, she was past listening to reason. It was all over.

Steamed Mom: one. Hot Girl: zero.

Julep let her backpack slide off her shoulder and onto the floor. Stalking past her mother, she trudged up the stairs. Halfway up, she nearly got run over by Cooper, who was thundering down the steps. The whole right side of his pale blond hair stood at attention. "Where are you going, Jules? I thought we were late."

"I gotta change."

He snickered. "Told ya."

"Shut up. You've got four Cap'n Crunch squares on your chin."

"I glued them on with milk. I'm saving them for recess."

"Mom's gonna—"

"She knows. Wanna see where I stuck the crunch berries?"

"No!"

Cooper's topaz-blue eyes flashed. "I'm telling mom you said shut up."

"Go ahead." She continued on her way up. "Add it to the list."

This was so typical. Julep wasn't allowed to wear her S.E. tee, but the human cereal bar got a free pass out the front door.

Julep's brother and sister got away with everything. Julep's fourteen-year-old sister, Harmony, was popular, beautiful, smart, athletic, and talented. She was in the ninth grade at Snohomish High School. Harmony was, among other things, a JV cheerleader. Big woo. Julep didn't know why everyone treated cheerleaders differently, like they had some sort of super-power or something. This morning, Harmony had pranced into the kitchen wearing three layers of Sizzle Red lipstick and a white denim miniskirt so tight a Barbie doll would have had trouble squeezing into it. But did Julep's mother say a single thing about *that*? Nope.

Huh.

Maybe Harmony did have a superpower after all: parental mind control.

In her room, Julep wrestled out of the plum T-shirt. She balled it up and chucked it into the Black Hole. Her father had named Julep's closet the Black Hole, noting how stuff mysteriously got sucked into it never to be seen again—things like her souvenir Tigger bracelet from Disneyland, last year's social-studies book, a cheetah-print scarf, and one of a pair of tuxedo cat socks her grandmother had given her (Julep had, in her defense, found the other sock behind the dryer).

Furious, Julep stomped in a circle. This was a complete injustice. Wrong, wrong, and in every sense of the word, wrong. She was not a baby. She was eleven years old and perfectly capable of selecting her own wardrobe.

Flinging open the bottom drawer of her dresser, Julep began tossing shirts and sweaters in every direction. About to thrust her battleship-gray, authentic Irish, hand-knit sweater skyward, suddenly it dawned on Julep what was really happening. Clutching the sweater to her chest, she rose to her feet.

Things were beginning to make sense.

It wasn't her mom's stressful job that was to blame for what was going on. Nor was it the tight spandex shirt or the adorable swish of gold words. Her mother had gone nuclear because she didn't want to admit that Julep was grown up enough to make her own decisions. If she acknowledged that, then she would have to stop controlling Julep's every move. She would have to trust Julep.

Horrors!

No matter what her mother said, Julep knew she *was* old enough to decide what she should and could wear. And nobody was going to stop her from doing just that.

Rescuing the HOT GIRL tee from the Black Hole, she shook it out and threw it on over her head. A few minutes later, Julep glided down the stairs wearing her gray, hand-knit sweater with the wide sleeves that fell a good three inches past her fingertips. For the past two years, her grandmother had been insisting that Julep would eventually grow into the sweater she had brought back from Ireland for her. Not a chance. There was still room to fit two, maybe three, NFL football players in the thing. Perfect-o!

". . . I couldn't let her wear that to school." Already on the phone to Aunt Ivy, Julep's mother was cradling the phone against her shoulder. "Don't worry. I'll return it for something sensible."

Translation: something hideous.

"Hmm. Maybe something in a toasty brown? She *looooooves* brown."

She haaaaaates brown.

Not that anyone ever asked.

Julep collected cereal boy from in front of the television and headed for the door. Gracefully, she swept past her mother and tossed the two stringed tassels on her sweater, which you were supposed to tie at the top of the V-neck, over one shoulder. Her mom raised one eyebrow as if to ask, "That's a pretty thick sweater for March, isn't it?" But all she whispered was, "Have a good day."

"I plan to," clipped Julep, her chin in the air.

Julep wore her HOT GIRL shirt to school. And she did it without disobeying orders. After all, her mom had forbidden her to be "seen" in the S.E. tee. So Julep simply kept her thick sweater on over the shirt so that no one would actually "see" her in it. It was a brilliant move, except that by the end of first period, Julep really *was* a hot girl—temperature-wise.

Springtime and chunky wool sweaters do not mix.

But the suffering was worth it.

Julep was tired of being told what to do. She had her own thoughts, opinions, and ideas. She had her own way of doing things. Why couldn't her mother understand that all Julep wanted was . . .

All she wanted was . . .

. . . what?

Julep didn't know. Still, she had a voice, even if she wasn't certain yet what she wanted to say.

A tiny bead of sweat trickled down the back of Julep's neck.

When Mr. Wyatt turned to write their math homework assignment on the whiteboard, Julep ripped a blank page out of the back of her notebook. She folded the piece of paper into an accordion and began fanning herself.

Air. She needed air.

Her bell sleeve fell down for the hundredth time that morning. Angrily, Julep pushed it back up to her elbow. She was mature enough to make her own decisions. And she was going to prove it to everybody. The sleeve slid down again. One hundred and one. If becoming independent meant sweating to death inside an enormous, gloomy-gray sweater that fifty sheep somewhere in Ireland had given their precious wool for, well . . .

Julep shoved her sleeve up.

. . . so be it.

2   A Killer Bee

The word is *colonies*," said Mr. Lee. "The thirteen British colonies won their independence in the Revolutionary War. *Colonies.*"

"*Colonies.*" The most popular girl in the sixth grade gently tugged on a long, black lock of hair that ended in a corkscrew curl. In a new baby-pink shirt with long, see-through chiffon sleeves, a pair of white jeans, and white sandals imported from Italy, Danica Keyes seemed to float before their English class like a dreamy cloud.

Julep gazed down at her own gray, floppy sleeves. She, on the other hand, looked like a pile of wet cement.

Inside her hand-knit sweater it had to be at least three hundred fifty degrees. Julep was being roasted alive. She seriously considered taking off the portable oven. Wouldn't that be something? Julep could show off her amazing HOT GIRL shirt, and her mother would never even know. It would be the most daring, most independent thing she could possibly do. But Julep didn't do it. And it would be a long time before she would admit why.

"Colonies," Danica said louder.

"Any day now." Trig's breath tickled Julep's ear.

Danica had placed a palm on each of her hip pockets and was turning in a slow circle. Her fourteen-karat-gold anklet with the ballerina charm reflected a beam of sunlight directly into Julep's eyes. It took Julep a minute to blink away the spots dancing in front of her.

Trig grunted. "It's a spelling bee not a beauty pageant."

Danica swung around and shot him a look that said if he'd been a little closer she'd have kicked him in the shins with her fancy Italian sandals.

"Come on, Danica," called Betsy Foster, a.k.a. Gosling Number One.

"You can do it," cheered Jillian Winters, Gosling Number Two. The pair began clapping.

Long ago, Trig had dubbed Danica "the head goose," and her three best friends "the goslings." The nicknames fit perfectly. Watching Betsy, Jillian, and Kathleen trail behind Danica down the halls of Heatherwood Middle School, you couldn't help but picture a line of baby Canada geese following their mother.

Kathleen O'Halleran, Gosling Number Three, started applauding, too, though she was on Julep's team. Nobody was surprised by this. It was an unwritten rule: Popular people always rooted for one another even when placed on opposite sides. Plus, it was common knowledge that Kathleen was, well, a few fries short of a Happy Meal.

"Col-oh-nies. Col-uh-nies?" Danica was obviously looking for a hint from Mr. Lee.

Their teacher gave her a neutral smirk to indicate she was on her own.

Suddenly a volcanic burp ricocheted off the walls. It was Trig, naturally, making an editorial comment about Danica's stall tactics.

Every boy in the class hooted.

Every girl cringed.

As if hit by a poison dart, Danica clutched her heart and staggered against a desk.

"I didn't know one of Trig's burps could kill." Julep giggled to Bernadette, who was in front of her.

A curtain of mocha hair swung around. "If only."

"Mr. Maxwell," warned their teacher, "another outburst will cost your team two points and you a little one-on-one time with Mr. Wilcox."

"Yes, sir," Trig said, shrinking into his white sweatshirt. He pulled his Seattle Mariners baseball cap down tight over his salsa-red hair. Whenever he got in trouble or wanted to charm someone, Trig's Kentucky accent mysteriously thickened. He'd start using a lot of ma'ams and sirs. Trig always knew just how far to push things, and how to charm his way to safety.

Danica, now recovered from the trauma of the earth-shattering burp, gave her soft, black hair one final tug and announced, "I'm ready."

"It's a miracle," mumbled Bernadette.

"My butt's asleep." That was Trig.

"So is your brain." Bernadette again.

"At least I have one."

"Butt or brain?"

Julep's two best friends in the world were constantly bickering, quibbling, tussling, and teasing each other. It was simply their way of communicating—a weird way, true, but it worked for them. Neither would ever admit how much they liked the other. But they didn't have to. It was obvious in the way Trig would lift Bernadette's pack from her shoulders when she'd step off the school bus coughing from yet another bout of bronchitis. Or how Bernadette would quietly slip a quarter into Trig's palm when he came up short for lunch.

Danica cleared her throat. "C-O-L . . ."

What was this—a pause?

For once in her life, was the all-powerful, all-fashionable head goose uncertain?

The class inhaled. The goslings fidgeted.

Trig clicked his tongue against the roof of his mouth, mimicking the tick-tock of a clock.

". . . O-N-I-E-S." She rushed through the last five letters. "*Colonies*. Am I right?"

"Correct." Mr. Lee signaled to Laura Frewer, who stood at the whiteboard. Laura made a mark in red pen for the red team.

Danica did a ballet leap, stuck her tongue out at Trig, and pirouetted her way to the back of the line to receive victory hugs from her two goslings minus one. Kathleen remained with the blue team, though you could tell by the look on her face that it was killing her not to be with her own species.

Julep took the opportunity to stretch out the V-neck of her stuffy sweater to let some steam out.

Ahhhhh!

"Smitty." Mr. Lee motioned toward Julep's team. "You're up for blue."

Smitty Feltis wore caramel-colored corduroys and short-sleeved plaid shirts to school almost every day. His overgrown hair was the color of a mud puddle in December. And, for some bizarre reason, he always smelled like a pot of baked beans. Even so, the kid was a genius. At lunch, he was always tinkering with a robot, glider, or remote-controlled something-or-other. Like most everyone in the sixth grade, Julep ignored Smitty Feltis. She had no choice. It was one thing not to belong to Danica's select group. It was quite another to be labeled a foser (female + loser = foser), which is exactly what would happen if she started being friendly to Smitty the Goser (guy + loser = goser).

It wasn't very nice, but hey, nobody said life was nice.

Mr. Lee surveyed his list of words, trying to find a tough one to challenge Smitty. "Here we go." He gave the class a devilish smirk. "*Rancor.* Her rancor was apparent by her cold words and stiff manner. *Rancor.*"

"*Rancor.*" Smitty clasped his hands behind his back. "I believe it's from the Latin *rancere,* meaning stinking smell or offensive flavor or bitterness. In other words, to stink. Of course, in English we use it to mean ill will—"

"Smitty, quit rancoring up the place and spell, will ya?" Calvin Kapinski taunted from the red team.

"Hey," called Robbie Cornfeld from behind Trig. "No yelling at the speller."

"*You* yelled," Calvin shot back.

"Not at the speller."

"Trig burped," said Danica, sticking out her lower lip.

"Technically, that's not a yell," corrected Trig.

Suddenly everyone on the blue team *was* yelling across the room at everyone on the red team and vice versa.

Mr. Lee put up a hand up to signal they had until the count of five to settle down or he would start handing out detention slips. Immediately they obeyed.

"R-A-N-C-O-R." Smitty rattled it off. *"Rancor."*

"Yes!" Julep clapped heartily until she saw Bernadette shaking her head. Bernadette's eyes were down, and she was slowly braiding the ends of her waist-length hair. No one else on their team was applauding. Julep's hands froze in midclap. Embarrassed, she let them fall to her sides. When Smitty's caramel corduroys swish-swashed past her on their way to the end of the line, Julep was fiddling with the tasseled cords on the front of her sweater and staring out the window at a row of green Dumpsters.

Next up was Millie Aldridge for the red team.

While Millie struggled to spell *champion,* Bernadette leaned toward Julep. "Check this out," she whispered, opening the side pocket of her knee-length, navy cardigan.

"You didn't?" gasped Julep, peering in.

"I did." Bernadette's deep brown eyes twinkled behind a pair of rectangular, gold wire-rim glasses. Carefully, she lifted out her new camera cell phone. "You have to get one, too, so we can call each other whenever we want and swap photos. Wouldn't that be fun?"

Julep touched the metallic purple phone. "Sure, but . . ."

She didn't finish the sentence. What was the point? In her head, Julep could already hear her mother's disapproving voice listing all of the reasons why her middle child shouldn't have a phone:

- They are too expensive.
- You'll talk to your friends instead of practicing the piano.
- You'll lend it to someone, and they'll call their cousin in Zimbabwe.
- You'll forget to take it out of your jeans, and it will go through the wash cycle.
- You'll drop it, sit on it, or lose it.

Julep clamped her hands over her ears. She didn't want to hear anymore, even if it was coming from inside her own head.

Why couldn't she have a mom like Bernadette's? Dr. Reed (Bernadette's mom was a pediatrician) didn't see the problem in letting Bernadette make most of her own decisions. She seemed to have faith in her daughter. Julep would give her entire bank account, all $347.22, to hear her mother say, "Julep, I trust you."

She'd have a better chance at becoming one of Danica's goslings.

"We can look at cell phones when my dad takes us to the outlet mall this weekend," hissed Bernadette, slipping the phone back into her sweater pocket. "He's going to give me fifty dollars to spend any way I want. We can buy some S.E. tees."

"Actually, Bern—" Julep started to say she hadn't yet asked whether she could go to the mall, but Mr. Lee was calling Bernadette's name. Millie had made a mistake on her word.

Bernadette calmly walked to the front of the room. "C-H-A-M-P-I-O-N. *Champion*."

"Show-off." Trig chuckled as Bernadette waltzed past. Still, he whooped it up with the rest of the blue team when Laura put up a point on their side on the board. Glancing behind her, Julep saw Smitty applauding. She wondered why he would bother to clap for people who never even acknowledged his existence. Julep wouldn't have done it.

After Robbie Cornfeld correctly spelled *medium*, Mr. Lee turned to Laura Frewer at the whiteboard for an update on the score.

Laura counted up the marks. "Thirteen to thirteen."

Their teacher glanced at the clock. Twenty-eight heads did the same. There were only five minutes left in second period.

Five minutes until Julep could get a drink of water and race outside to let the spring breeze cool her sizzling body. She couldn't wait.

"We are out of time," said Mr. Lee. "Whichever team is the first to misspell a word loses the bee. Oh, and did I mention, the winners won't have to take the vocabulary quiz tomorrow?"

An excited murmur rippled through the room.

"Sudden-death spelling," said Trig. "I like it."

Looking directly at Julep, her teacher crooked his finger.

"Me?" A hand flew to her chest.

It couldn't be her turn already, could it? She had been the last person in line. It was her favorite spot. Whenever they divided up into teams for a spelling bee, Julep always made certain to take the last position so she'd only have to spell once. If the other students were particularly slow, sometimes Julep wouldn't have to spell at all. It wasn't because she was an awful speller. She was pretty good, actually. No, the problem was that whenever Julep got nervous, her body totally betrayed her. First, her eyesight would go fuzzy. Then her stomach got woozy. Not long after that, her brain started to ice over. At that point, she would be fortunate to even recall the ABCs, let alone spell any difficult words in front of the head goose, the goslings, and the rest of the class.

Fuzzy, woozy, and icy.

It was not a good recipe for success, which is why Julep avoided spelling as often as possible. Quickly, she glanced around. Mr. Lee wasn't teasing. It *was* Julep's turn. Licking two parched lips that were getting drier by the second, Julep peered over her shoulder. A line of hopeful faces stared back. The blue team was counting on her. Her fate was sealed. Today, she was going to have to do it. Julep was going to *have* to spell.

Her vision already starting to blur, Julep could make out Betsy Foster on the other side of the room. Gosling Number One was at the head of the line for the red team, wearing a buttercup-yellow S.E. tee that read LITTLE ANGEL (so not the truth). Betsy was bouncing on her toes, eager for Julep to screw up so her team would win. Strands of red beads resembling Red Hots dangled from each ear. The lines of Red Hots bobbed against her shoulders with each hop. Betsy always wore pierced earrings that were big, swingy, and colorful. Julep wished she could have pierced ears, too, but with a mother like hers, it wasn't going to happen anytime this century.

Julep felt Trig's hand on her back, nudging her forward.

All eyes were on Julep as she inched her way to the center of the room. She clung to the tassels of her big, gray sweater as if they were rip cords on a parachute and she was falling out of the sky at a million miles per second.

"Julep, the word is *typhoon*," said Mr. Lee. "In the Atlantic Ocean, a severe storm is called a hurricane, while in the Pacific it is known as a typhoon. *Typhoon*."

"Ty . . . typhoon?" Julep swallowed past the growing lump in her throat.

Why did she have to be the deciding one? WHY?

What kind of sick person would make a game out of spelling

out loud? This was no game. It was torture. Pure torture. There ought to be a law against spelling bees in public schools. But there wasn't, so Julep took a deep breath and forced herself to do what she dreaded most in the world.

"T . . . Y . . ."

It was Y wasn't it? Oh gosh, maybe it was an I-E.

It was too late to take it back. She would have to keep going.

Julep was ninety-nine-point-nine percent certain this was one of the words where the F sound was made by the letters P and H. Even so, a tiny bit of doubt was doing a triple back flip with a half twist in her stomach.

Closing her eyes tightly, she pressed onward. "P . . . H . . ."

Julep was just thinking how odd it was that her voice sounded as if it were coming from across the room, when a strange sensation washed over her. Her body felt feverish, but her hands and feet were cold. Worse, Julep couldn't remember what word had been rolling around on her tongue only a second ago. Or why she was here. Or her name.

Oh, rats! It was happening.

Brain freeze. Her mind was beginning to separate from her body.

Feeling her shoulders sway, Julep opened her eyes. ". . . O . . . O . . . O . . ."

Julep was still clutching her tassel rip cords, though she knew they could not save her. There was no parachute on her back. She was free-falling out of control, plunging toward Earth at top speed. Soon she would hit the ground with a horrible *splat* and make a big mess out of everything. As the temperature soared beneath her sweater, Julep began to feel very much like a baked apple. She liked baked apples—the way the cinnamon and brown sugar melted into the warm, mushy sweet meat of the apple. Yum.

Wait, why was she thinking about apples?

"Focus," her brain reminded her as it drifted upward and bumped into the ceiling. "You were spelling, remember? Keep spelling."

". . . O . . . O . . ."

"Julep?" Mr. Lee's head floated in front of her. "Are you okay?"

". . . O . . ."

This word sure has a lot of Os.

". . . O . . ."

Does it smell like cinnamon in here?

There was no time to answer before Julep's world went dark.

"She's dead."

"She is not dead."

"How do you know she isn't?"

"How do you know she *is*?"

"It's that sweater," said a dreamy cloud in white, Italian sandals. "Gray makes everyone look dead."

"Mr. Lee, if Julep's dead, can I have her desk by the window?"

"Calvin."

"I'm saying *if* she's dead."

"If she's dead, do we win?"

"Betsy!" That was Bernadette.

"Well, it's not like we have to wait for her to officially finish. Everybody knows *typhoon* does not have six Os in it."

The bell rang, signaling the end of second period.

Nobody moved.

"Julep? It's Mr. Lee. Julep, can you hear me?"

"I'll bet she's gone to the light."

"What light?"

"You know, heaven."

"Oooooooo," moaned a concerned chorus.

"She's coming around," said Mr. Lee. "Everybody stand back."

Everybody crowded in.

After all, how often do you get to see one of your classmates come back from the dead?

Julep's eyes fluttered. The circle of faces huddling around her went in, then out, of focus. When her gaze found a familiar one, she motioned for him to come closer. An ear lowered itself to within inches of her lips so Julep could murmur her final words to Nelson Gibbs before going to the light.

The moment he lifted his head, the class pounced on Nelson.

"What did she say?"

"I'm not sure, but"—Nelson scratched his chin—". . . I think she said, 'No more pictures.' "

Dear Journal:

I am now a complete FOSER (female loser). And it is all M.M.F.
(see decoder page). Here is how it all happened:

Julep wants to wear new
self-expression tee
(a perfectly reasonable request).

Evil mother says, "I forbid
you to be seen in that!"

Julep overheats in
sweater and passes
out during spelling bee!
(Trust me, you do
not want to see a
drawing of this!)

Julep must wear HUGE gray
sweater over S.E. tee so
she won't be "seen" in it.

27

IT'S OFFICIAL!

Bernadette called tonight to see how I was doing, but my mom said I couldn't talk because I'm still on phone restriction. Can you believe that? I almost died of S.S. today.

> C.Y.L.,
>
> Julep

P.S. I am still trying to come up with a cool name for you. Hang in there!

Julep's Decoder Page

KEEP OUT!   PRIVATE STUFF!

M.M.F.: My Mother's Fault

S.S.: Sweater Suffocation

C.Y.L.: Check You Later

TRESPASSERS WILL BE FED MY MOM'S SEAWEED SOUP

(trust me, it's deadly—my dad uses it

to kill the dandelions in our yard)

3   BUTTERFLY KISSES

Cautiously, Julep slid out her underwear drawer. When the gap between the drawer and the dresser was about six inches, she dove for cover behind the corner of her bed. Her heart skipping more than a few normal beats, she peered out from between the white, wooden slats of her bed frame. She waited for a good minute, but nothing happened.

Strange.

Leaning back, she stretched out a leg and stuck her bare foot under the drawer knob. Gingerly, she pulled the drawer open a bit wider. Still nothing. Finally, Julep ventured out of her hiding place and went over to take a good look inside her underwear drawer. Very strange, indeed.

No rubber rodents. No fake barf. No uncooked macaroni noodles.

Something was terribly wrong. It had been nearly two weeks since Cooper had tried any of his tricks on her. Her pain-in-the-rumpus seven-year-old brother was way past due for a prank.

Julep scanned her room, her eyes coming to rest on the sky-blue satin box on her desk where she kept her favorite photos and other small souvenirs. The lid was slightly askew. Spotting her purple ruler on the desk, she picked it up and carefully moved toward the box.

"Aha!" she cried, using the end of the ruler to fling off the lid. Yet, instead of being grossed out by dead grasshoppers, Julep found herself staring at the usual assortment of postcards, photos, and mementos.

Everything was normal.

Still holding her ruler for protection, Julep turned to scan the clothes, games, toys, and stuffed animals that littered her closet. Surveying the Black Hole, she squished her lips up the left side of her face. Everything looked fine. Cooper wasn't usually this lazy when it came to tormenting her. He was probably hiding somewhere: calculating, plotting, planning, and waiting to make his move. He was letting her gain confidence, letting her think he wasn't going to do anything, and once she relaxed—*WHAM!* That's when he'd strike. Julep knew she would have to remain on guard. She would have to keep her eyes and ears alert at all times so he couldn't possibly take her by—

"Hey!"

"Yaaaaahhhh." Julep's feet fired her straight up into the air.

"Don't pop a cork," said Harmony, while her sister clutched her rib cage to make sure her heart hadn't exploded out of her chest.

"I thought you . . . you were Coop," huffed Julep.

"Overdue for an attack, huh? Mom and Dad really need to

do something about him. Did you see what he did with my new root-beer lip gloss?"

Julep shook her head.

"The toad used it to wax his Hot Wheels track. Mom and Dad totally let him off—again."

"It figures," said Julep, grabbing a pair of gray socks out of her underwear drawer. She sat on the edge of her bed to put them on. "What's up?" she asked, raising an eyebrow. It was rare for Harmony to set one dainty toe in Julep's room—unless, of course, she wanted something.

With the flick of her hand, Harmony tucked a piece of straight, honey-streaked blond hair behind one ear. "Dad's taking me to the dentist this morning, so I have time to French-braid your hair, if you want."

"If I want?"

For months, she'd been begging her sister to braid her hair. But Harmony had said that it would be less of a hassle to untangle the giant ball of ten thousand Christmas lights in their garage. She had insisted that no way, no how could she possibly control the mammoth waves of mutant hair that grew from Julep's head. So what had changed? Why was she, suddenly, so willing to do it?

Watching Harmony fidget in the doorway, Julep began to understand. Beautiful, talented, smart, and publicly adored Harmony Elizabeth O'Toole felt sorry for her frumpy, fainting failure of a younger sister. This, clearly, was a pity braid.

Julep searched her sister's face. "Is there anybody in the Northern Hemisphere she hasn't told?"

Harmony said she didn't think so. "But," she was quick to add, "Great-Aunt Lurlene is on her Alaskan cruise, so Mom could only leave a message."

Groaning, Julep fell backward on her bed and flung a hand over her face. Did her mother have to tell everyone about how Julep had passed out during the spelling bee? And, while she was sharing the gory details, did she have to be so happy about it? Her mother seemed to delight in humiliating her. Still, she wasn't as bad as Calvin Kapinski and his buddies, Eddie Levitt and Carl Stickney. For the past couple of days, every time the trio spotted Julep at school, they would pretend to pass out cold. It didn't matter where they were—in the main hallway, in the cafeteria, even outside on the sidewalk near the buses—the boys would sway back and forth and faux-faint (Julep knew a little French, thanks to Harmony, and *faux* meant fake). Calvin's performance was the most annoying of the three. He would roll his eyes up into his head, and go, "O . . . O . . . O," just the way Julep had done while trying to spell *typhoon*. Then he would clutch his heart and stagger around dramatically for a few minutes, before falling flat on his back.

SO not funny.

At first, Julep had been so mortified by their performances she had simply run the other way whenever she saw them coming. But she knew she couldn't hide forever. So the fifth time it happened, she stood her ground. When Calvin went into his fainting spell in the hallway of the science wing, she stared at the ceiling blankly like his performance was the most boring thing in the world. When he collapsed, Julep merely stepped over his limp body (taking the opportunity to drag her foot over his leg) and went on her merry way.

What a jerk and a half!

"Come on," said Harmony, pulling Julep off her bed. "Let's braid. You'll finally have some decent hair, and it'll take your mind off of . . . you know."

In the bathroom, Julep flipped through one of Harmony's teen magazines while her sister attempted to run a wide-toothed brush through her tangle of reddish-brown hair. One particular article caught Julep's attention. It was about a group of middle-school girls in San Diego who'd started a friendship journal. Each person in the group would write and/or draw in the book before passing it on to the next friend. The girls said that creating a friendship journal gave them a chance to talk about the things they might be too shy to discuss in person. It was also a great way to encourage one another, swap jokes, and just have fun. It certainly *did* seem fun to Julep. As she thumbed through the magazine, she heard the spritz of hair spray and the whoosh of mousse, punctured by the occasional "darn" from her sister's lips.

"Ow," cried Julep when something snapped her head back.

"Still, please." Two hands firmly clamped on to Julep's head and recentered it.

"What's going on back there?"

"Minor technical difficulties. Do you know you have alpaca hair?"

Julep snickered. She had never thought about it that way before, but her thick waves did resemble the soft, crimped fleece of the huacaya (wha-KY-yuh) alpacas on Aunt Ivy's farm. Last year, her aunt had begun raising alpacas on her thirty-acre farm in Birch Bay. Alpacas were smaller—and sweeter—cousins of llamas.

Julep loved Cloud Nine Ranch, where she got to feed and, if she was lucky, pet the timid alpacas. Cassiopeia had the most extraordinary thick fur—light gray on top, with a pinky-rose tinge on the crimped fur underneath. Sky Dancer, who was pure white, was always sniffing Julep's neck with his wet nose. There was Starburst, a fawn alpaca with a darker tan, star-shaped blotch on his side, and eight-month-old Wisteria, a buttery cream ball of fluff that would follow you anywhere for a handful of sunflower seeds. Dark chocolate-brown Fancy was mom to a newborn baby, called a *cría*. Julep had yet to meet the newest member of the herd, but she hoped to very soon. Cloud Nine was a place where everyone, animals and humans, loved you without limits. If Aunt Ivy hadn't lived two hours away, Julep would have been at the ranch every spare minute of her life.

"Finished," announced Harmony. She held up a round hand mirror so Julep could view her hair from every angle.

Turning, Julep saw two perfect braids woven tightly against each side of her head. The braids started at the top of her skull and ended in two little tufts of hair, one behind each ear. Harmony had wrapped a red elastic ponytail holder around the ends, making it look as if she had two tiny broomsticks brushing against her head.

"You look older."

"I do?" Julep fingered the ridges of hair.

"At least thirteen."

Thirteen? Julep straightened her back as Harmony coated her head with another layer of hair spray.

"You want some blush?" Temptation whispered in her ear.

"Blush?"

"Just a touch of Butterfly Kisses."

"I'd better not."

"It's light pink. Besides"—Harmony's ice-blue eyes met Julep's in the bathroom mirror—"Mom already left for work."

"You're sure it's light?"

"You'll hardly know it's there," promised Harmony, going for her makeup drawer.

Julep could barely stop squirming long enough for her sister to brush a hint of Butterfly Kisses on each cheek.

Harmony stepped away so Julep could look at her own reflection. "See? It's completely natural."

It was true. Julep didn't look much different, except for a slight rosy glow on each side of her face. If she hadn't felt the little brush swipe over her skin, she would not even have known she was wearing makeup.

Whoa! It is true. I'm wearing makeup. My first real makeup.

It was history in the making.

Julep couldn't wait to tell her journal all about it. She would definitely have to come up with a name for her most treasured friend soon. "Dear Journal" was just too dull.

"Girls?"

The hand mirror slipped from Julep's hand and bounced off her left foot before clattering to the floor. If there was pain, and there probably was, the shock of seeing her mother kept her from feeling it.

Harmony whirled around, hiding the evidence behind her back. "Mom," she squawked. "I thought . . . we thought . . . uh . . . we didn't know you were still here."

Their mother leaned close to the mirror to check her fuchsia lipstick. "Cooper has a sore throat. I'm staying home today so your dad can go to class."

Last summer, the software design company their dad owned had gone out of business. Bill O'Toole had decided to go back to college to become a secondary-school science teacher. Julep was fine with that, as long as he didn't end up being *her* science teacher. The last thing she needed was a parent at school every day, especially a parent that gave tests, homework, and detention.

"Cooper's sick?" Harmony confirmed.

The sisters exchanged relieved looks. They were off the hook, prankwise, for at least twenty-four hours.

"Harmony, don't keep your dad waiting."

"Right." She winked at Julep before breezing out of the bathroom, the small, round container of blush tucked safely in her palm.

"I've got to go, too," mumbled Julep.

Her mother put an arm across the door frame to block her exit. "Before you do, I want to talk to you about—"

"What?" Julep cut in impatiently.

Every time her mother wanted to "talk," it meant Julep was going to have to do all the listening. The "talk" usually involved making her do something she didn't want to do, go somewhere she didn't want to go, or try some kind of health food she didn't want to eat.

"I thought we'd go shopping tomorrow. Just the two of us."

"Oh." Julep forgot to hide her disappointment.

"What's wrong? You love the mall."

"The thing is . . . I mean, Bernadette's dad is taking her to the outlet mall in Burlington, and she invited me to go with them."

"I see." Her mother's face hardened. "Today is Friday. When exactly were you going to ask me?"

Julep twisted a braid. "When you weren't in such a nasty mood" was probably not the best answer. So Julep crossed her fingers and said what she always said in situations like this: "I meant to, but . . ."

The idea was to leave the *but* hanging, so to speak, and let your parents fill in the blank with whatever they came up with on their own. Of course, if pressed, Julep would finish with "but I had three tests this week and I was busy studying." That usually saved her.

Julep didn't understand why her mother was screwing up her lips that way. What was the big problem-o? It wasn't like their family ever had any major plans for the weekend anyway. Besides, she was asking now, wasn't she?

"So can I go?"

"Another time. I'm sure she'll understand."

Bernadette might understand. Julep never would. It was like her mother lived just to smash her dreams into a zillion pieces.

Julep's crossed fingers became two clenched fists. "I have to go," she clipped. "I'm going to be late meeting Trig."

Her mother dropped her arm to let her pass.

Julep had found one tennis shoe and was fishing around under her bed for the other when she heard a soft voice say, "Julep?"

Not again. What did her mother want now? It could be one of a hundred things, though the top three were:

1) When are you going to clean the Black Hole?
A: *You'll be the first to know.*
2) Must I always tell you to wipe the hair out of the bathtub?
A: *In case you hadn't noticed, I'm not the one with the long, blond hair.*
3) B's are fine, Julep, but don't you think you're capable of more?

There was no right answer to that one. If you said yes, they'd hold you to it, and if you said no, you ended up with an after-school tutor (Julep knew from firsthand experience).

"Are you"—her mother paused—"wearing blush?"

Julep let out a silent wail and pushed herself farther under the bed. She was thankful that the apricot polka-dot bed skirt covered most of her head and shoulders. If only she could stay here forever. It just figured, didn't it? Nobody in the known universe but her mother—old Eagle Eyes—would have spotted the faintest hint of pink on her cheeks.

Yet another dream shattered. Her mother was two-for-two today.

"Honey, you know the rule."

Julep knew it. And she hated it. The law was she couldn't wear any makeup until she was thirteen. Why thirteen? It didn't make any sense. Makeup was off-limits when she was twelve and 364 days, but the day she turned thirteen, suddenly it was acceptable? How ridiculous was that? Thirteen was a random number, and Julep was far more than a number, especially now that she was sporting two grown-up French braids, which, by the way, her mother hadn't even noticed.

Julep madly rubbed her left cheek against the carpet and her right cheek against the palm of her hand. She emerged from under the bed with her tennis shoe and two red, raw cheeks.

"I'm not wearing blush, Mom," she said flatly.

Not anymore.

"Don't get upset. I'm only trying to . . ."

A) Control me?

B) Keep me from growing up?

C) Drain every drop of fun out of my pathetic life?

The answer was always D. All of the above.

". . . look out for you the best way I know how," her mother finished.

Why was it that what was usually "best" for her from her mom's point of view was the exact opposite of what Julep considered "best" for herself. Leaning against her mattress to work the knot out of a shoelace, Julep could tell by the thoughtful look in her mother's eyes that she was about to launch into a lecture. Julep tugged like crazy, but the knot wasn't budging.

"You know, Julep, it's important to remember that true beauty comes from within."

"Uh-huh."

"It's not how you look on the outside that matters, but who you are on the inside."

"Uh-huh."

"If you have a good heart, that's the most important thing."

Julep was now gnawing at the knot with her teeth.

"That's what you should concentrate on—becoming a kind, bright, creative human being. Don't you see that? Don't you see that life isn't about clothes or make up? None of that stuff makes one bit of difference in the world."

Julep took the shoelace out of her mouth to ask, "Then how come you wear makeup?"

"Uh . . . well . . ."

She had her mom now.

"I mean, you know, if none of it matters like you say.

"It's because . . . I mean, I'm old enough to realize that it won't change me into someone I'm not. It's only a little color here and there."

Julep took in her mother's bold fuchsia lips, magenta-streaked cheeks, and charcoal-covered eyelids. "A little?" she murmured under her breath. "Puh-lease."

Mascara-clumped eyelashes blinked rapidly. "What?"

"Nothing." The knot in the lace, finally, came undone. Julep dropped her shoe.

Why bother? Nobody was interested in her point of view anyway. This was just one more contradiction in a long line of dumb, confusing rules. It was okay for her mother to slather on five coats of makeup, but let Julep try to get out the door with barely a wisp of Butterfly Kisses, and it was a crime against humanity.

Her mother let out a weary sigh, clasped her hands together, and stalked out of the room—to get a couple of aspirin, no doubt.

Julep shoved her feet into her tennis shoes. Leaning over, she yanked the right lace as tightly as she could. Why couldn't her mother let her wear a tiny bit of blush this one time? Why couldn't she forget about her silly rule simply because she loved Julep and understood how much this meant to her? After all, she met most of her mother's standards for being a good person on the inside. What was the harm in allowing her to look nice on the outside? Couldn't you do both? It was S.N.F. Bernadette's mother let her wear glitter rose blush, lavender eye shadow, and berry lip gloss to school *every* day. What Julep needed was an extreme mom makeover.

Who do you write to for something like that?

Julep was tying the bow of her left tennis shoe when she felt it—a warm, gooey sensation penetrating her sock. Quickly, she loosened the lace. She pulled out her foot to discover a long, orange tube of ooze wrapped around her toes.

Cheez Whiz.

Julep let out a screech. "Cooper!"

4 Fitting Room of Doom

ou're awfully quiet." Julep's mother glanced over at her daughter slumped in the passenger seat. "Is anything the matter?"

You mean, other than the fact that right now I could be at the outlet mall eating Hawaiian pizza and trying on great clothes with Bernadette, but instead am being forced to return my HOT GIRL shirt for something brown and "sensible"?

"Nope."

Her mother pulled their red minivan into a parking space, set the brake, and reached into the backseat. A plastic bag crinkled at her touch. They both knew the silver bag contained a certain banned self-expression tee that was going back to the store where Julep's aunt had bought it less than two weeks ago.

Julep wished Aunt Ivy were here right now. She could really use someone on her side, someone who listened and understood what it was like to be eleven years old. Her aunt visited about once every four months or so—not nearly enough. Of course, Aunt Ivy had the alpacas to look after and couldn't easily get away. Not that Julep blamed her. If she lived in a glorious place like Cloud Nine, she'd never want to leave it, either.

Her mother was holding the silver bag in her lap. "You're still upset about this, aren't you?"

"No," said Julep firmly. She would not give her mother the satisfaction of seeing how much this was killing her.

You might as well face it, O'Toole. You will never be admired. You will never be a fashion diva. You will never be so important that the paparazzi will stalk you for your photograph. What you will be is . . . is . . .

Brown.

Very, very brown.

"I hope you finally understand why we need to return this," her mother was saying.

Julep did not understand. "I don't see what's wrong with it," she said.

"Then maybe you could trust me this time."

Trust you? Why should I trust you when you don't trust me?

As usual, she squashed the question before it left her brain and got to her lips. Instead, she shrugged and said, "Whatever."

"Julep, why do you have to make everything so hard?"

Quickly, Julep lowered her amber eyes and blinked back a well of tears. She didn't mean to be difficult. But none of this was her fault. Her mother was the one refusing to accept that Julep was mature enough to make her own choices. *She* was the one making everything so hard. However, that was one of those taboo thoughts to be shared only with her journal.

"You can stay here and mope, or"—her mother leaned over the steering wheel to gaze out the windshield—"you can go inside with me to pick out something else. It's your choice."

She glanced at her mom sideways. "You'd let me choose?"

"Yes."

"Anything I want?"

Her mother let out a sarcastic laugh that meant "no way."

Julep threw her head back against the seat. "Then tell me the rules. What *can't* I have?"

Her mom held up a finger to signal she needed to think. Then, after a minute: "Here's what you can't have: nothing with words on it, unless it's your name."

"Acceptable," said Julep crisply. Now it was her turn. "Nothing brown."

"Nothing too sheer."

"Nothing brown."

"Nothing that shows your belly button—or anything else, for that matter."

"Nothing brown."

"Nothing that costs more than twenty-five dollars, and that includes the return."

"Nothing—"

"I know." Her mother's lips turned up at the corners. "Nothing brown. Ready?"

"Ready." Julep flung open her door.

Let the shopping begin.

———

"How's it going?" Julep's mother was trying to peek over the pink doors that separated them.

"One sec." Julep turned left, then right, in front of the rectangular mirror. Two red, satin sleeves poofed outward and upward. It looked like she was carrying an enormous tomato on each shoulder.

"What do you think?" Julep's mom pressed.

"I don't like it."

"How about the green one with the daisies? That was nice."

"Too tight," lied Julep.

Daisies were babyish. They were clearly not for a girl on the verge of womanhood who had worn French braids and a touch of Butterfly Kisses blush.

"Do you want a bigger size in the red?"

"No!" Julep fell against the back wall of the tiny dressing room.

This was a nightmare. Why was it she could go to one store with Aunt Ivy and come across tons of incredible stuff, yet shop all day with her mother and find squat? For more than two hours, Julep had been trying on shirts in every size, shape, and color: poet blouses, tank tops, crewnecks, turtlenecks, tunics, V-necks, short-sleeved tees, long-sleeved tees, and on and on and on. But if Julep loved it, her mother hated it. And vice versa. If, by some freak of nature, they both agreed on a top, it was either too expensive or bore the dreaded "dry-clean only" tag.

While she struggled to escape the tomato shirt, Julep's stomach let out a fierce gurgle. She was hungry. She was tired. She was an emotional wreck. Julep didn't even want a shirt any-more. The only thing she wanted to do was go home and pig out on sour-cream-and-onion potato chips.

"Mother!" Julep shrieked when her mom started to open the doors. "I'm naked from the waist up."

Her mom chuckled. "I'm the only one here."

That was SO not the point.

"Could I have some privacy, please?" Julep held the doors shut. Absently, she reached for the next shirt. Sure, it was okay for her mother to expose Julep to the entire world, but let Julep do the same to her mom and she'd be grounded for life. Parents made you follow rules they didn't think twice about breaking.

This is definitely the last one, Julep told herself, yanking an-other shirt off its hanger. First, she accidentally stuck her arm through the neck hole. Once she located the correct armhole, Julep pulled the top down over her stomach only to discover it was on backward. It took a half minute or so to fix that little problem. And when, at last, she had her head and arms where they properly belonged, a starving, frazzled, defeated Julep glanced up into the mirror and saw herself.

She let out a gerbil cry.

Could this be a hunger mirage?

Thin rows of soft, pastel stripes ran horizontally over the front of the stretch, cotton-knit shirt. The colors gently driz-zled into one another the way shades of pineapple, orange, and raspberry blend to create a luscious fruit sherbet. Starting at

47

the shoulder, a line of small heart-shaped cutouts traveled down the center of each long, tapered sleeve, revealing little glimpses of pale, freckled skin beneath. Julep tugged on two peach suede drawstrings to pull the scooped neck a bit tighter in front. She tied the string into a little bow, then slid a fingertip over the white, ceramic-heart beads attached to the ends. Julep whirled in front of the mirror, and a line of peach suede fringe trim at the hem happily swung with her.

It was sweet, yet sophisticated. Darling, yet dramatic. Simple, yet stylish.

The top was, in a word, perfect.

Spinning in her white, ankle socks, Julep hugged herself.

"Julep, do I need to send in a search party?"

She stopped, suddenly, in midspin.

Julep adored the pastel-striped shirt, which automatically meant her mother was sure to dislike it. Julep sighed and took one last twirl to see the hearts dance down her arms and watch the fringe sway. At least she'd gotten to wear it for a few blissful moments. Determined to get the rejection over as quickly as possible, Julep stepped out of the fitting room. Her mother, lounging in a wingback chair nearby, straightened up. Two brown eyebrows flew to the top of her forehead.

"Isn't it great?" gushed Julep.

"It's, uh . . . uh . . ."

Suzanne, the college-age salesgirl who'd been helping them, came around the corner carrying an armload of jeans. "Oooh," she cooed, catching sight of Julep. "The peach tones really bring out the golden highlights in your hair."

Highlights? I have highlights? Where?

Suzanne was nodding. "I think we've found *the* one."

Julep beamed. "Me, too."

"It's certainly"—Julep's mother was looking at the trail of cutout hearts and the freckled skin peeking through—". . . different," she finished. Her sour lemon expression indicated she meant "different" in a bad way.

"It is a distinctive look," pointed out Suzanne. "Not everyone can wear it, but she's got the body for it."

"I do?" blurted Julep, inspecting her pancake chest, straight hips, and stick arms in the big mirror. According to Harmony, Julep didn't have a body at all, to speak of.

"Sure, with those slim hips and swanlike neck . . ."

Whoa! No one had ever referred to her neck as swanlike before. Once, Calvin Kapinski had called her "spaghetti legs," but that was about it. Swans were beautiful. Swans were graceful. Was Julep really graceful? Just think what everyone at school would say when she glided into class wearing this. Just think how Danica and the goslings would react to something, and someone, so glamorous.

"Julep, you look so graceful," Danica would gush. "Don't you think so, too, Betsy?"

"Very swanlike."

"You should be a ballet dancer," Danica would insist, flashing

her ankle bracelet with the tiny ballerina on it. All of the goslings would eagerly agree.

"Well, I was . . . I mean, I used to take lessons at Miss Pauline's School of Dance," Julep would inform them, neglecting to mention that she had, as Harmony bluntly put it, "flunked out."

But now that she had the pastel shirt everything would be different. Once Miss Pauline saw how elegant Julep looked in it, she would beg her to come back to class. Julep would become the best ballerina in the school's history. She would arabesque and pirouette and port de bras (that was where you moved your arms gracefully) her way to international fame. When she danced, an audience would be moved to tears. They would shout "bravo!" and throw hundreds of Joseph's Coat roses at her feet, even in winter. Julep would be admired by millions. The best part was that, in her entire charmed life as a prima ballerina, she wouldn't faint—not even once. And it would all happen because Julep's understanding mother had let her buy the most wonderful shirt in the world.

Julep *had* to have the shirt, or she'd die right here and now.

"Mom?" she begged.

Her mother was chomping on her lower lip. "I don't know."

Astonished, she moaned. "What's not to know?"

Sensing a bit of tension building, Suzanne scurried to take her stack of jeans to the front.

"It's exactly what I've been looking for. I love it, Mom. I really, really, *really* love it."

"It's awfully grown-up."

Didn't her mother get anything? That was exactly *why* Julep really, really, *really* loved it. Julep's mind was racing. She had to persuade her mother to let her buy the shirt. But how? Julep would do anything, go anywhere, and even eat anything wretchedly healthy that her mother cooked if it meant she could own it. "I'll do extra chores for a whole month," she began to plead. "I'll do my homework the second I get home from school. I won't fight with Harmony or Cooper, even if he pulls a stupid prank. I'll clean my closet and pull weeds and vacuum the den and—"

"The Black Hole." Her mother's eyes widened. "You'd clean the Black Hole?"

Julep bobbed her head so hard her neck popped. "So can I have it?"

Her mother blew air out of her cheeks. She stroked her chin. She crossed and uncrossed her legs. Three times. Then, at last, she spoke. "What are the cleaning instructions?"

There it was!

It was barely a hairline crack in her mother's resolve, but it gave Julep hope.

Julep fumbled for the tag. "Hand-wash cold, drip-dry," she said triumphantly. No dry cleaning. One hurdle down.

Come on, Mom. Say the magic word.

"How much is it?"

Fumbling for the tag, Julep groaned when she found the price. "Thirty-two ninety-five," she confessed. Returning the

HOT GIRL shirt had given her sixteen dollars and change. Julep had promised her mother that she would not go above twenty-five dollars for a new shirt, including the return. "Wait," she cried, before her mother could destroy another dream. "What if I paid the difference out of my allowance?" Julep clasped her hands together. "Please, Mama. *Pleeease?*"

"Well . . ."

Say it.

"This must mean a lot to you if you're willing to do extra chores and . . ."

Say it.

". . . avoid fighting with your brother and sister and clean your closet . . ."

If you don't say it I'm going to spontaneously combust.

". . . and pay the difference."

SAY IT!

A gentle grin smoothed the kinks out of her mom's mouth. "Okay."

Julep leaped into her mother's arms, nearly knocking her to the floor. "Easy now." Her mom laughed, trying to steady them both.

"Thanks, Mom." She planted a bunch of kisses on her mom's cheek. "Thank you, thank you, thank you."

"You're welcome, you're welcome, you're welcome. Now go change. I'm starving."

"Me, too," called Julep, skipping back into the fitting room and shutting the pink doors.

"Where should we go? The Bean Blossom Café or Nature's Pantry?"

Julep stuck her tongue out at her own reflection. When your mom is a vegetarian and eats strange food like tofu, soybeans, and chickpeas, you're pretty much stuck eating it, too. Normally, Julep would have protested, but right now she was too happy about the shirt to bother. Why, she could probably even down a stick of kelp jerky, which tasted like truck tires rolled in salt, and not even flinch. Julep was determined that nothing— NOTHING—was going to spoil this day.

Carefully, Julep slipped out of the pastel shirt and placed it back on its hanger. She stroked the peach fringe. Soon it would be hers! Julep had to do a little dance around the tiny dressing room to release her joy.

". . . clothes are so important to girls."

"Maybe too important," said Julep's mom. "I wish my fourteen-year-old paid more attention to her schoolwork and less to her appearance."

Julep could hear her mother and Suzanne chatting outside the dressing room. She grabbed the steel-blue cotton shirt she had worn to the mall off the hook. Putting it over her head, she stuck her arms through the short sleeves, pulled it down, and tucked it into her jeans.

"They are in such a hurry to grow up," said Julep's mom.

"I suppose we all were at that age," said Suzanne.

Julep pushed her feet into her tennis shoes and tied the laces at warp speed.

"It seems like only yesterday I was walking my pigtailed little girl to kindergarten in her oversize raincoat and galoshes, and now—well, did you see her in that top?"

"She looked very grown up. How old is she?"

"Eleven. Any day now, she'll be sprouting breasts, and we'll be back here arguing about what kind of bra to buy."

An arm in her sweater, Julep froze. Slowly, she turned toward the doors.

No. *No!*

She refused to believe her ears. Her mom had not just said—

Yeah. She did. Your mother just discussed your nonexistent chest with a complete stranger. Worse, she used the word sprouting.

The blood rushed into Julep's head so fast her ears started to ring. Even so, the shrill noise pounding her skull could not drown out the women's giggles. Her sweater slid off her arm and onto the floor. She sank down onto the little pink padded bench attached to the wall. How could her mother have said such a thing? Julep was never going to forgive her. Never! And she was certainly not going out there to face the two of them so they could keep laughing at her.

Glancing around, Julep felt her breath quicken. She began to panic as the realization hit her: Julep was trapped in the Limited Too dressing room with no way out.

Okay. Okay. This is not a problem. You will just live here for the rest of your life.

Sure. Live here. Makes perfect sense. You'll order out for pizza. A lot of pizza.

Was she out of her mind? Of course, Julep would have to leave, and when she did, Suzanne and her mother would be waiting to embarrass her again. Why did adults think puberty was so funny? Just because they had been through it, and you hadn't, that didn't give them the right to tease you about it.

Besides, most of the girls in Julep's class weren't any more developed than she was. Nearly everyone in PE, including Julep, wore camisoles or tank tops under their shirts, not bras. There were two types of girls who wore bras: those who needed them and those who pretended they did. Danica wore a bra (just for show). Laura Frewer wore a bra (needed it). Betsy, Jillian, and Kathleen also wore bras (show off, show off, and show off). Julep had thought about getting one, too, of course. She might want one next year. Maybe sooner. But no matter what happened, or more important, *when* it happened, it wasn't the kind of thing your mother was supposed to make fun of, with a stranger, no less! How *could* she?

Julep's scalp started to itch, and her humiliation began morphing into outright anger. It felt as if the pink walls were, suddenly, shrinking around her. She was tired of her mom taking pleasure in humiliating her. Julep wasn't a little girl anymore. Why, she was nearly a teenager, and it was time to stand up for herself.

Setting her lips tight, Julep picked up her sweater off the floor and put it on. She flattened her hair against her head, though her waves sprang back to their original form the moment she lifted her palms. Julep set her graceful shoulders back and lifted her swanlike neck as high as it would go. Then, punching through the swinging doors, she marched out of the fitting room. Without a word, she stalked right past her mother and Suzanne.

"Julep?"

Head high, looking neither left or right, Julep continued on her way.

"Where are you going?" called her mother. "The shirt—"

"I don't want it," she yelled, zigzagging her way to the front of the store.

"What? Julep, wait a minute. *Wait!*"

But Julep did not wait for a minute, not even a second. She had only one thing on her mind: getting out of the mall as fast as possible. And that is exactly what she did.

Her mom, finally, caught up with her on the sidewalk outside the food court. "Julep, stop!" A hand clamped onto her forearm. "What is wrong with you?"

Julep shrank away.

"Why did you run out of there like that?" her mother said loudly, attracting the attention of a group of high-school girls walking past.

If her mom was that clueless, Julep was certainly not going to enlighten her, especially in such a public place. She turned away to run her finger along the side of a concrete planter.

"Did you change your mind about the shirt? Are you delirious with hunger? What *is* the matter?"

The more questions her mother hurled at her, the angrier Julep got. The angrier she got, the more determined she became not to speak. Instead, Julep began rapidly yanking the petals off a dead pansy.

"You're not talking to me now, is that it?"

Julep let the petals fall to the cement.

"This is great." Her mother tipped her head back. "Just great. I have had about enough of this attitude of yours, Julep. If you aren't muttering something under your breath, you're not speaking to me at all. How am I supposed to know what's going on if you won't talk to me?"

"I do talk. You don't listen," Julep mumbled to the pansies.

"What did you say?"

Julep shook her head.

"Julep Antoinette O'Toole, you are in serious trouble."

Allison Constance Gallardo-O'Toole, so are you.

She didn't say it, of course. But she desperately wanted to.

"Come on," clipped her mom. She began digging in her purse for her heart key ring. "If you aren't going to say anything, there's no point in staying."

She was giving her daughter one last chance to set things right. Julep knew that. Yet she didn't know what she was supposed to say. One minute she'd been planting kisses all over her mother's cheek, and the next they were fighting outside the food court. How had things gone so wrong so fast? Julep was furious and embarrassed, but more than anything, she was hurt. When so many painful emotions are tumbling inside of you, sometimes you don't know what to do to fix things. You only know you want to cry, and that's all you know.

Her mother slapped her keys against her thigh. "Fine. Let's go home," she said, her jaw clenched.

Julep wanted to say she was sorry.

But she didn't.

She wanted to beg her mother to please let her go back for the pastel shirt.

But she didn't.

Exhausted, Julep did the only thing she could think to do. She followed her mom into the parking lot. Julep made sure to keep her head low so nobody, especially her mother, could see the tears rolling down her cheeks.

12:39 P.M.   Mood: Restless

Dear Journal:

I went shopping with my mom yesterday. W.A.N.! It was THE WORST day ever. You are SO lucky you don't have a mother.

You're not going to believe what my mom said to the salesgirl about me while I was changing (don't even try to guess). It's too ghastly to write. Anyway, I got mad and ran out of the store. I had to leave behind the M.B.S.U (see below). Major bummer.

Today, I called Aunt Ivy and begged her to let me come to Cloud Nine for spring break. I told her Mom and I had a C.F., but I didn't share the details. She said it was okay with her, and she would talk to my mom about it. Thank goodness, because I cannot even look at my mother right now. I have to go to Aunt Ivy's! I <u>have</u> to get out of here and away from <u>her</u>!

Nothing is going right. We started a new unit in PE last week: square dancing! C.M.L.G.A.W.?

I have to go. My mother is yelling at me to practice the piano. I hate piano (I know I've told you this a billion times so thanks for letting me say it again).

I need some Milk Duds in a big way.

C.Y.L.,

Julep

Ta-da!

Here it is: the most beautiful shirt in the universe. Don't get attached. It isn't mine. Sigh!

Julep's Decoder Page
GO AWAY!

W.A.N.: What A Nightmare!

M.B.S.U.: Most Beautiful Shirt in the Universe (sigh)

C.F.: Colossal Fight

C.M.L.G.A.W.: Could My Life Get Any Worse?

WARNING!

IF YOU'RE SEVEN YEARS OLD, YOUR NAME IS COOPER, AND YOU ARE READING THIS, PREPARE FOR DEATH BY TICKLING!

5 A One-Girl Revolution

Sprouting? She really said sprouting?"

"Bernadette!" Julep hid her face in her hands. "Tell the entire cafeteria, why don't you?"

"Sorry." Her co-best friend glanced around to make sure no one of importance, such as Danica Keyes or, heaven forbid, Calvin Kapinski, was nearby. They weren't. She lowered her voice to say, "I am in a state of complete amazement."

Julep peered through her fingers. "Welcome to my life."

"So what did you do?"

"I got out of there as fast as possible."

"You left the shirt?"

"I had to."

"Too bad." Bernadette was doing her best to spread a glob of peanut butter on a cracker using the little red stick that came with the packet, but it wasn't going well.

"She honestly didn't know why I took off. She didn't get it."

"They never do."

It was sweet of Bernadette to sympathize, but she truly had no idea what Julep was going through. Bernadette's mom and dad were divorced, and she lived with her mother. In every way imaginable, Dr. Reed was the exact opposite of Allison Gallardo-O'Toole. Whenever Julep spent the night at Bernadette's, Dr. Reed would let them make their own banana splits, leave them alone to dance or watch TV, and allow them stay up as late as they wanted. In contrast, when Bernadette came to sleep over at Julep's house, her mom fed them homemade prune bread (gag-o-matic), was constantly poking her head in Julep's room to check up on them, and made them go to bed promptly at 11:00 P.M. A real party mom. *Not.*

Julep doubted Dr. Reed ever got tension headaches brought on by headstrong eleven-year-old daughters. She'd certainly never heard her make up dumb rules. Bernadette got to think, eat, and wear whatever she wanted. Today, she had on a new tangerine S.E. tee that her dad had bought for her at the outlet mall. It said PAMPERED PRINCESS.

Julep and her mom had barely seen each other since their fight at the mall over the weekend. Her mother had spent most of Sunday at a picnic to raise money for the museum, and this morning, she'd left early for work. Julep wasn't avoiding her mother, but she wasn't seeking her out, either. She had the feeling her mom was probably doing the same thing with her.

"I know she's waiting for me to apologize," Julep told Bernadette. "But it wasn't my fault. Why should I say I'm sorry when I didn't do anything wrong?"

"It's always our fault, even when it's really their fault," said her co-best friend, giving up on the stick and using her finger to spread the peanut butter.

Julep opened her lunch bag to take out a bagel stuffed with goat cheese and alfalfa sprouts. Staring at the white goop and squiggles of grass oozing out of her bagel, she lost her appetite. How many times had she told her mother goat cheese gave her a stomachache?

"Heads up," Bernadette hissed across the table. "The Monster is coming."

Mrs. Flaskin was the lunch monitor, though lunch monster was a more accurate description. Wearing one of her calico-print dresses, her large body would slowly toddle between the rows of tables. She was supposed to keep an eye on the kids to make sure they behaved. Of course, one eye was all she had (the other was glass). As she shuffled down each aisle, the Lunch Monster's good eye roved back and forth, rooting out any unprotected junk food. If she locked on to you, you might as well give up your fries, chips, Tater Tots, pudding, Jell-O, or cupcake, 'cause nobody survived Mrs. Flaskin's liver breath. She snacked on dog treats. Snausages, mostly, or so the legend went.

"You poor thing," said Bernadette. "First, you had to take back the HOT GIRL shirt, and then you lost the pretty pastel top. So not fair."

"It was almost mine," Julep said dreamily, the memory of the soft peach fringe still fresh in her mind. "I was minutes away from owning it. If only my mother hadn't said it."

"Said what?" A mint-green tray with three cheeseburgers and a mound of potato wedges clattered against their table. Trig slid into the seat next to Julep.

Julep gave Bernadette a horrified look. Normally, she could tell Trig most anything, but this was definitely one of those "girls only" topics. While a red-faced Julep began stammering and tearing through the plastic wrap on her bagel, Bernadette jumped in with, "Julep couldn't go to the outlet mall with me this weekend 'cause she had to clean her closet."

Trig gasped. "You cleaned the Black Hole?"

"Yeah . . . that's right . . . well, I'm working on it," she said, still flustered. Julep mouthed a thank-you to Bernadette.

"Look for my moose key chain, will you," Trig said.

"And my pearl barrette," added Bernadette.

"Okay," said Julep, watching as Trig stuffed half a cheeseburger into his mouth at once.

Bernadette rolled her eyes. "That is the most disgusting thing I've ever seen."

Viewing this as a challenge, Trig parted his lips to reveal a blend of mashed-up beef, cheese, pickles, ketchup, and bread. Bernadette had to admit she had been wrong. "Now that is the most disgusting thing I've ever seen," she corrected herself. "You are so crude, Maxwell."

Trig had to swallow his megamouthful of food before he could retort with, "Says the girl who spreads peanut butter on a cracker with her finger."

A yellow-and-white floral blob floated behind Bernadette,

making gaspy, whoosh sounds the way a hot-air balloon does when it's trying to lift off the ground. But this was no hot-air balloon. When Mrs. Flaskin's curly, carrot-top head swiveled in their direction, Julep latched on to her bagel and began nibbling around the outside of it. Trig stuffed the other half of his burger into his mouth and covered his tray with his upper body. Bernadette licked the last of the peanut butter off her index finger and clamped her hand over her bag. The Lunch Monster paused a moment, glanced at them, and then moved on. Nobody at the table relaxed until she was a full three rows away.

A wary Bernadette popped the top off her strawberry-mango yogurt. "Did you ask your mom about getting a cell phone?"

Julep gave her friend an annoyed look that said, "What do you think?"

"You've got to ask soon, okay? It's not any fun unless you have someone to call," she whined, sliding the purple phone out of her pocket. "Or someone calls you."

Bernadette placed the camera phone in the center of the table. The three of them stared at it as if, simply by willing it with their minds, they could make the thing ring.

After a minute, Bernadette said, "See? All it does it sit there."

His mouth full of potatoes Trig asked, "What do you want it to do. Sit up and beg?"

Ignoring him, Bernadette began stirring her yogurt. "Julep, do you want to come over after school today and help me make popcorn balls for my Campfire Girls meeting tomorrow?"

"Can't. Piano lesson."

"That's right. I forgot. Hey, I thought this was the year you were going to quit."

"I was . . . I am." Julep pretended to do an in-depth search of her lunch bag to find something. Anything.

"She says that every year," snorted Trig.

Julep pulled out a low-fat chocolate pudding cup. "I mean it every year."

But, somehow, she never seemed to do it.

Six years ago, Julep's mother announced that it was "high time" her youngest daughter learned to play the piano. High time turned out to be that following Monday afternoon. That's when Julep's mom picked her up from kindergarten and dumped her at Mrs. Pahtoshnik's brick house on Kaleidoscope Way. Since then, every Monday after school Julep had ridden her bike to Mrs. Pahtoshnik's for her piano lesson. She had tried to force herself to like it, but it hadn't worked. Julep had disliked the piano from the very beginning—the way her fingers got cold when she played, the endless scales, and the hours and hours of practice it took to master something as basic as "Three Blind Mice."

Occasionally, over the years, Julep had tried to tell her parents she didn't want to take piano anymore, but all she got ever got for her effort was the same lecture. "Stick-to-itiveness," her mother would say, "is the key to overcoming things when you're a bit discouraged."

Julep wasn't "a bit discouraged." She was flat-out, completely uninterested.

This year, Julep had planned to ask her parents if she could learn to play the trumpet instead, and join band. Bernadette was in band. She played the oboe. But positive that her parents would say no, Julep had avoided asking. Besides, as long as she didn't ask, then a sliver of hope remained that her wish might come true. Of course, merely hoping for a trumpet didn't get you one. It bothered her that no one had ever thought to ask what instrument she had wanted to play in the first place. Julep was beginning to think that it was "high time" her opinion counted for something.

"Sorry," Julep said to Bernadette. "I'd give anything to skip piano."

A wicked grin slithering across his jaw, Trig hungrily glanced from Julep's pudding cup to Bernadette's phone and back to the pudding again. "You mean it?"

Julep could practically see the neurons firing in his brain. She knew what he was up to. Trig was daring her to dare him to get her out of her piano lesson. Normally, she would have laughed it off and told him no way was she going to risk getting into trouble.

However, today was different. After everything that had happened with her mother over the past several months, including this past weekend, Julep was feeling more frustrated than ever. Her inner strength seemed to be draining away. A week ago, Julep had overruled her mother and worn the S.E. tee to school under her sweater. She had vowed to fight for her independence. She had promised to take a stand for her freedom. Yet what had she done since then? What had she accomplished?

Zippo. Zero. Zilch.

Nothing in her life had changed. In fact, things were getting worse.

If she didn't do something soon, who knew what the future would hold for her?

A picture of herself as an adult flashed in her mind. Julep was hunched over Mrs. Pahtoshnik's grand piano playing Beethoven's "Ode to Joy" for the ten billionth time. She was wearing a shapeless brown burlap dress, brown kneesocks, and a brown bow in her hair. It was a colorless world without makeup, pierced ears, or high heels. Julep shook the image from her head, and with two fingers, she pushed the pudding cup over to Trig.

The contract was sealed: one chocolate pudding for one piano vacation day.

Trig picked up Bernadette's phone and dialed the number Julep gave him. On the outside, Julep remained steady, but on the inside, her organs felt like they were ping-ponging all over the place. She had never defied her parents before. Well, she had, but not when it came to something as sacred as piano lessons.

Bernadette, her spoon poised in midair above her yogurt,

could only watch in awe. It was obvious she had not expected Julep to do something so drastic.

The clock on the wall behind Trig caught Julep's attention. She should have known. Eight minutes was his limit for staying out of trouble, and he'd been at their table for ten. Suddenly the reality of what was about to happen smacked her in the face. Maybe this wasn't such a good idea, after all. Her mom was still pretty upset about the incident at the mall. Julep could always take a stand for her independence at a more convenient time, say, next week. Or even the week after that . . .

Julep reached for his arm. "Trig, I don't think this is such a—"

"Mrs. Pahtoshnik?" Trig's voice was raspy and deep. "This is Julep O'Toole's father. She won't be able to make her piano lesson this afternoon because . . . because . . ."

Unaware that she was dripping yogurt on the table, Bernadette gaped at Julep.

Numb, Julep could only stare back.

Trig rarely lost his cool. If he messed this up, she would be doomed for sure.

". . . uh . . . her parakeet died."

Bernadette dropped her spoon.

Julep dropped her confidence.

A moment later, Trig clicked off the phone.

Julep attacked. "What did she say?"

"Nothing." Calmly, he dipped a potato wedge in ketchup.

"Nothing?" Julep brightened.

"I got her machine."

Julep started munching off the fingernails on her right hand.

Bernadette shook her head. "You couldn't have said something normal like she had a cold?"

"Never question the master, Reed," Trig said, his Kentucky accent thickening. "Relax, Julep. I know what I'm doing. With a dead pet, she's not going to call your mom to check up on you the way she would if you were sick. Trust me, you're home free."

Julep wasn't so sure. She didn't have Trig's gift for staying out of trouble. Trouble seemed to Velcro itself to her at every turn. But if she *could* get away with it this once, that would be something. That would prove something, wouldn't it?

That afternoon, as she did every Monday, Julep hopped on her bike and rode down the teeth-jarring, gravel path behind the school. She passed Trig, who was crossing the parking lot to pick up Cooper at Valley View Elementary and walk him home, just as he did every Monday.

Julep yelled and waved.

Trig raised a hand. "Have fun," he shouted.

"Don't tell Cooper," she called.

He cupped his hand to his ear. "Huh?"

"Don't tell Cooper where I'm going."

Trig was shaking his head. He hadn't heard her. She would have to trust that her co-best friend would be wise enough not to tell her bigmouthed little brother what she was up to. If he knew, Cooper would tattle on her for sure.

Julep turned right out of the parking lot and pedaled down Bayview to hang a left on Kaleidoscope Way. But instead of going straight four blocks, she turned right on Calypso Drive. Bernadette also lived on Kaleidoscope Way, which meant Julep had to go three blocks out of her way around Mrs. Pahtoshnik's house to avoid being spotted by her piano teacher or any of her students. Coasting toward Bernadette's, the wind fluttering through her hair, Julep was already feeling different. For the first time in her eleven years on the planet, she was doing exactly what she wanted to do when she wanted to do it. There was no one to tell her she wasn't smart enough, trustworthy enough, or old enough to think for herself. For once in her life, nobody was holding her back.

Julep felt energetic. She felt powerful. She felt, at long last, totally free.

"Wa-hoo!" Julep shouted her revolutionary call, raising both arms high into the air as she flew down Suicide Hill.

7:57 P.M.   Mood: Happy, happy, happy!

Dear J:

No piano lesson today! No scales, no frozen fingers, no metronome going tick—tock, tick—tock until I want to rip my ears off. Trig gave Mrs. P.'s answering machine his dead—pet story, and she bought it. She didn't even call my parents to check up on me. T.A.F.L.U!

Of course, it's only one day off of piano, but I feel as if it is the beginning of something BIG. I am becoming a freethinking girl. Just imagine, if I could escape from P.P., think what other stuff I could do.

Other stuff I could do:

Ride a unicycle

Learn to speak French

(that's French for "yes")

Spell without fainting

Play the trumpet

Wear an S.E. tee

Buy a camera cell phone

Eat MEAT!

The possibilities are endless!

What would I do without you? You are always here for me. You never judge me, you never criticize, and you don't make dumb rules. You just listen. You are T.B.F.E.! Parents could learn a lot from you journals!

By the way, I've come up with a list of names for you:

Priscilla	Lucy
Catherine	Sandra
Mandy	Beulah (after my great-great-grandmother)

See anything you like?

Good night, my dear friend!

C.Y.L.,

Julep

Julep's Decoder Page
NO PEEKING!

T.A.F.L.U.: Things Are Finally Looking Up

P.P.: Piano Prison (of course!)

T.B.F.E.: The Best Friend Ever

DO YOU HAVE WRITTEN PERMISSION FROM
JULEP ANTOINETTE O'TOOLE TO READ THIS?
I DIDN'T THINK SO!

6 Do-Si-Don't

"**D**on't llamas spit? I thought they spit."

"Bernadette, they're *not* llamas," said Julep, tipping her head to the right to stretch out the left side of her neck. How many times did she have to say it? "They're alpacas."

"Yeah, but do they spit?"

Julep let out a squeal, but she wasn't really mad. In fact, she was quite the opposite. Everything was all set with Aunt Ivy. Julep was going to spend five days at Cloud Nine Ranch during spring break, and Bernadette was coming, too.

"Side stretches," called the lanky woman in a navy sweatshirt and matching sweatpants. The elasticized cuffs came about five inches short of a pair of bright yellow socks, revealing two white shins that had probably never spent a day at the beach.

Their PE teacher, Mrs. Springborg, had come to be known throughout Heatherwood as, simply, the Borg (as in *Star Trek: The Next Generation*'s "resistance is futile"). She was merciless. It didn't matter if you had the flu, sore muscles, or bubonic plague. When the Borg was on duty, nobody sat out of PE. Nobody, that is, except Trig Maxwell. Julep didn't know how he did it, but somehow, the smooth-talking charmer could break through, or maybe melt, the Borg's iron skin. In fact, he was at the front of the gym right now, trying to weasel his way out of their square-dancing unit. Julep wondered what he'd come up with this time. She had a feeling it was probably something with an *itis* on the end like tonsillitis or appendicitis.

Bernadette shifted her upper body over her right leg. As she stretched, her dark brown ponytail slid over the floor. "The la-pacas better not spit on my glasses. That's all I'm saying."

"*Al*pacas," corrected Julep.

She wished her co-best friend would quit with the spitting thing. Once Bernadette met Cassiopeia, Wisteria, Sky Dancer, Starburst, Fancy, and the new *cría*, she would instantly fall in love with their deerlike faces, soft fleece, and gentle personali-ties. "They might spit at one another if they're really angry, but they hardly ever spit at people," she said, hoping her explana-tion would put an end to Bernadette's obsession.

Julep leaned as far over her right leg as possible and reached for her toes, but did not bounce into the stretch. Apparently, bouncing was bad for your muscles, though no one had ever told them *why*. If the Borg caught you bouncing, it was five laps around the gym. So nobody bounced.

When they had completed their stretches, the Borg blew her whistle. "Boys line up along the wall." Their teacher's voice boomed off the high ceiling. "Girls line up on the opposite side in front of the bleachers."

The class scurried to obey.

Trig sauntered over to where Bernadette and Julep stood. "Excuse me." He slipped between them, a cocky expression on his face. Trig bounded up the bleachers and took a seat on the end of the fourth row. Locking his hands behind his head, he leaned back and crossed his ankles.

"What is it this time?" Bernadette asked drily.

"Flat feet." Trig wagged his tennis shoes. "My doctor says I can't dance."

"Your doctor's right," said Julep. "You can't dance, but it has nothing to do with flat feet," which, she knew for a fact, he did not have. Trig's feet were as normal as hers (three sizes bigger, true, but normal).

"One of these days, the Borg is going to realize that you and your 'doctor'"—Bernadette made a pair of invisible quotation marks in the air—"have the same signature."

"Until then . . ." He turned to lie flat on his back. Repositioning his baseball cap over his face, Trig folded his arms across his chest, closed his eyes, and pretended to snore.

The girls took off their sweat jackets and threw them on top of him. He didn't even flinch.

"Did you ask about a cell phone yet?" Bernadette wanted to know as they got in line.

"Uh . . . no."

"What are you waiting for? Everybody's getting them."

In her head, Julep heard her mother's voice chime, "You are not everybody."

She shook it off.

"You're going to be left out," said Bernadette. "Danica got one yesterday."

"Yeah? Then call her." Julep was tired of being badgered about the whole thing.

"Let's go." The Borg was motioning for the head of each line to come toward where she stood in the middle of the gym. Suddenly it dawned on Julep what they were doing. For the last few classes, the students had spread themselves out across the gym floor. Alone, they had learned and practiced the different square-dancing steps. Despite their objections (and there were many), the Borg had told them that the day and time were coming when they were going to have to dance together—boys and girls. Cooties.

That "day" had come. And that "time" was now.

Double cooties.

The heads of their respective lines, Millie Aldridge and Robbie Cornfeld had the unfortunate tragedy of being the first couple to be paired up. When Robbie neared the center of the gym, he hesitated.

"Take her hand," ordered the Borg.

Robbie's neck turned four shades of red.

Millie dropped her head. She refused to look up. She stuck her arm straight out. Robbie did the same. Somehow, the two of them managed to catch hands.

Kids whooped and whistled.

"Go Millie." Danica laughed, clapping. The goslings standing behind her quickly joined in. Millie and Robbie raced down the centerline as if being pelted by eggs.

"Come on, step it up." The Borg signaled for the next two people to link hands in the middle of the gym and head for the back wall. "Nobody's going to bite."

Julep snorted out loud. She knew for a fact that Calvin Kapinski *did* bite.

Please, God, don't let me get paired with Calvin.

Suddenly the race was on to figure out who you were going to get stuck with. Frantically, Julep counted back from the head of her line to discover she was tenth in line. She looked across the gym, trying to count ten back from Danny Dufrain to see who she would get as a partner. But she was so nervous she kept losing her place. Worse, it was becoming impossible to count accurately because many of the girls had started changing places to get better positions. The boys were doing the same thing. Nobody wanted to get stuck with a goser or foser. It was a mad scramble. Betsy cut in front of Julep. Danica cut in front of Betsy. You knew it was bad when the head goose and her goslings were jostling with one another.

"Bernadette!" Julep cried out as someone spun her around. In the confusion, the two friends had gotten separated. Somehow, Bernadette had been pushed to the front of the line, while Julep had been thrust toward the back. Still dazed, Julep hugged the bleachers and watched Bernadette get matched up with Rodney Philapart (a.k.a. Rodney Pick-apart due to his nose-picking and snot-flicking abilities).

Rodney held out his hand for her. Everyone, including Julep, groaned in horror.

Shaking her ponytail, Bernadette locked her palms together with her fingers so she wouldn't have to take his hand. As she walked down the center of the gym beside him, the look on her face said she was all too aware that eventually, she was going to have to touch those snot-encrusted fingers.

Julep let out a grateful breath when she saw Calvin was next in the boys' line. She was glad for herself but sorry for his partner, Laura Frewer. She was going to have her hands (and her feet) full. Calvin would be cracking jokes and screwing up the dances on purpose.

While her attention had been focused on Calvin, Julep did not notice that Betsy and Danica had slipped in behind Kathleen, pushing Julep to the back of the line. She no longer had to count backward to figure out who she would be paired up with because, obviously, the last girl in the girls' line got the last boy in the boys' line. She squinted to see who she would . . .

Uh-oh.

Abort. Abort!

Disaster ahead.

If you don't so something fast, you're going to get . . .

Julep shivered. Her brain couldn't even process the possibility.

Casually, but quickly, Julep attempted to slip into an open space in front of Kathleen, but got a sharp elbow in the side for her effort. Her desperation growing, she tried to move between Danica and Betsy; however, the girls weren't having any part of it. They put up their forearms and glued their hips together so she couldn't wedge them apart.

Betsy gritted her teeth. "No chance, underpants."

Rubbing her bruised ribs, Julep had no choice but to go back to her old place at the end of the line behind Danica.

Before gliding to the center of the gym to be paired with Peter McVickers (the most popular boy in the sixth grade), the most popular girl in the sixth grade turned to Julep and whispered, "Sorry. But *somebody* has to dance with him."

That somebody, they both knew, could not possibly be Danica. It simply wasn't acceptable for middle-school royalty to be seen in the vicinity of gosers.

And so it was that Julep O'Toole, the very last girl in the girls' line, stumbled across the freshly waxed, hardwood floor of the main gym to meet—even from ten feet off he smelled like baked beans—the very last boy in the boys' line: Smitty Feltis.

"Didn't you want to turn to vapor the very second you saw him?"

"Uh-huh." Julep opened her carton of soy milk and stuck the straw in.

"Did you ever think that in a hundred million years you would have to do something so gross?"

"Huh-uh."

"I mean, Rodney's bad enough." Bernadette twitched her

nose to push her glasses up. "But Smitty must have been a total cootie experience with extra fleas on top."

"Shhh." Julep nodded toward where Smitty was sitting a few rows over. He was bent over his latest creation—a tall, wooden pyramid. On the bench beside him teetered a Nike shoebox filled with all kinds of screwdrivers, wrenches, and other tools.

Bernadette lifted a shoulder as to say, "Sorry, but he must know he's strange."

Sipping her milk, Julep pretended to be looking out the window behind Bernadette, but she was really watching Smitty. He was at the end table in the last row, sitting alone. As usual. He was smoothing a corner of the triangle with a raggedy piece of sandpaper. Julep figured the pyramid was about eight to ten inches tall. It didn't look like a robot or anything that could be remotely controlled. What it was supposed to be?

Ordinarily, Julep would have agreed with Bernadette about yesterday's square-dancing experience. She *had* wanted to evaporate the second she'd gotten stuck with Smitty Feltis, Goser of the Century. Never in a hundred million years did she think she would have to do something so gross. And, yes, she had prepared herself for the "cootie factor" from the first moment her chilled fingers had made contact with his sweaty ones.

But then something unexpected happened.

Smitty, who didn't fit in with anybody anywhere in the universe, turned out to be a pretty good square dancer. Smitty knew all the steps, including the do-si-do, a tricky move where a couple has to circle each other. To begin, each partner takes a step forward and slightly to the left so you pass right shoulders. Then you have to step to the right so you are back-to-back, and then you step backward, passing left shoulders to return to your original starting place. Not once during the do-si-do did Smitty bump into Julep or step on her heel. The grimacing faces of Millie, Laura, and Betsy told her they weren't fairing as well with their partners.

A couple of times, Julep got confused about which way to promenade (that's where you walk side by side with your partner around the circle counterclockwise). Swinging to the left, instead of the right, she promptly crushed Smitty's foot.

"I'm sorry." Julep grimaced.

"It's okay." He chuckled. "I've still got one left."

"I get turned around and keep forgetting which way to go."

"To the right," he whispered. "Since you're always on the right side of me, whenever the Borg calls 'promenade,' tell yourself we go *your* way."

"Got it," said Julep.

After that, she never messed up again.

As the period came to a close, the Borg instructed, "Bow to your corners."

While Smitty bowed to Millie on his left, Julep turned to acknowledge the boy on her right, Nelson Gibbs. The school photographer had gotten Betsy Foster for a partner. She had done nothing but spend the whole time criticizing the size of his feet. They were, in all honesty, huge—almost twice the size of Julep's. Of course, it wasn't like Nelson had much control over it. She felt sad for him, having to listen to Betsy's constant complaining.

"How long is this unit?" Nelson mumbled to Julep as they bowed.

"Uh . . . eight more days."

"I think I feel an eight-day cold coming on," he said, faking a sneeze.

Julep laughed.

"Bow to your partner!"

Julep and Smitty swiveled to obey the call from the Borg and bonked foreheads. Rubbing their sore skulls, they both smiled. The pair had managed to get through the last forty minutes without injuring each other only to end up smacking heads on the very last move.

"That's all," sang the Borg, turning off the music. "Hit the showers, people."

"Is your head all right?" Smitty asked her.

Julep said it was. "Yours?"

"Fine." Fumbling with the bottom of his T-shirt, Smitty seemed unsure what to do with his hands now that the music was over.

"Well . . . okay, then." Julep trotted backward toward the bleachers to get her sweat jacket. "See ya."

"See ya." With a shy wave, Smitty started toward the boys' locker room. He didn't see Calvin scurry up behind him. Julep watched Calvin kick the back of Smitty's ankle.

"Look who's got a flat tire?" mocked Calvin.

Everybody stopped to look, and laugh, at Smitty, who was limping in a circle, trying to get his heel back into his tennis shoe.

Boys could be SO immature sometimes. Bernadette said it was because they ate too much junk food, and the sugar stunted their development. Julep didn't know if that was true, but considering Calvin frequently washed down four Hostess Ding Dongs with two cans of orange soda for lunch, she was willing to consider the possibility that Bernadette might be right.

"Julep?" Trig was snapping his fingers in front of her to bring her back to reality.

"What?" Julep reached into her lunch bag for her sandwich.

"For the third time, did your parents find out about your piano vacation day?"

"No," she said, trying to smile. "Everything went perfectly. Thanks."

Hiding behind her dolphin-safe tuna-fish sandwich, Julep stole another glance at Smitty. Now that she knew him a little better, she didn't think he was such a goser, after all. Once you got past the overgrown hair and all that corduroy, he was actually kind of nice. That was more than you could say for certain popular people who wore T-shirts with silly sayings scribbled on them, and who pushed everybody around.

Julep watched Smitty carefully blow some dust off his wooden pyramid. She wondered what clever invention he was working on this time. She wondered if Smitty took notice of the lively conversations and laughter going on just beyond the invisible walls of his workshop. She wondered if it bothered him that everyone thought he was too weird to even bother speaking to. Julep wasn't sure about the first two questions, but you didn't have to be a genius to figure out the answer to the third.

All you had to be was one freethinking girl.

7 Bombs Bursting in Air

Julep's nose caught a whiff of baking squash and immediately quivered, proving her theory that it was called squash because you had to squash up your nose to inhale the odor. The stale smell always reminded her of a jack-o'-lantern that had been left out too long after Halloween.

Even so, Julep was determined that nothing, not even a pan of squaccoli (Julep's nickname for her mother's premade, frozen squash-and-broccoli casserole now bubbling away in the oven) was going to detour her from her mission. Operation Cell Phone was about to get under way. Bernadette wasn't the only one who could get her parents to give her cool stuff.

Julep slid a taffy-yellow place mat next to the open book on the kitchen table. "Dad, wouldn't it be great to be able to get ahold of me whenever you needed to?"

Her dad held up his finger to signal he was almost finished reading the page.

Her timing was perfect. His body was in the room, but his mind was far away—a good sign that he might say yes without fully realizing it until after the mission was complete. And, as even a three-year-old knows, once a parent says yes, it's officially carved in marble. They can't take it back.

"You know, Cooper and I have to walk through the park every day on our way to and from school," she said softly into his ear. "It can sure be dark in there, especially on rainy mornings like today."

He put up a second finger.

Julep circled her father, setting the place mats around the dining-room table. "Besides, it's always good to be close to the phone in case of an emergency. In case somebody tries to kidnap you or something."

At that, his head came up. "What?"

"That's why I was thinking . . . I mean, a lot of kids at school are getting—"

Bam!

The kitchen door flew open so hard the doorknob smacked the wall behind it. Julep swung around. Her mother was holding the screen door open with the toe of her black pump. She shook out her red-and-green plaid umbrella on the back porch. "Sorry, I'm late. It's raining like crazy out there. There was an accident near Northgate, and traffic was backed up to the ship canal bridge." She dropped her briefcase at the door and dumped the mail on the granite countertop.

Julep's shoulders sagged. She was hoping to get her dad to go along with the cell-phone idea before her mother could torpedo it.

Mission delayed.

She would have to try again later. Julep went to get the plates out of the cupboard while her father took the squaccoli casserole out of the oven.

"So what's new?" asked her mother, coming back into the kitchen after hanging up her coat. She unclipped her tortoise-shell barrette. Thick reddish-brown hair, tinged gray at the temples, fell to her shoulders.

"Not much," said Julep's dad. "Julep wants a cell phone."

"I do not," clipped Julep, startled that she had been caught in the act of dad wrangling. She strolled around the table, setting each of the five plates on a place mat. Watching her mother out of the corner of her eye, Julep noticed that her mom wasn't rubbing her forehead or tipping her head back in that way she did when she was stressed-out. Instead, she was flipping through the mail and . . .

Was that humming?

Hello! Operation Cell Phone calling.

"Since you brought it up, Dad," Julep said, "some of the kids at school do have them."

"You mean, Bernadette has one." Her mother smirked, opening an envelope.

Julep stuck her right hand inside the cuff of her left sleeve. "She might."

Her dad had pulled out the retractable faucet and was washing a head of butter lettuce in the sink. "Do you know what having a cell phone costs, Julep?"

"Not exactly."

How bad could it be? After all, Bernadette's camera phone was soooo tiny.

"You have to buy the phone first, then, of course, there's the monthly bill, which is more than your allowance."

Hold the phone. More than her allowance? Did they actually think that *she* was going to pay for it?

Turning off the water, her dad shook off the lettuce and set it on the cutting board to pat it dry with a clean dishtowel. "While I am in school we all have to be more aware of what we spend and how we spend it."

"I know, but—"

"So what is the one question we ask ourselves in any situation involving money?"

At that, Julep let out a combination groan and sigh—a grigh, actually. "Is this purchase really vital to my existence?"

The answer, of course, was . . .

Yes! A cell phone was absolutely critical to staying out of foser-ville.

"She doesn't need a cell phone," her mother said to her father. She turned to Julep. "You're eleven. Who would you possibly call?"

Julep's mouth fell open. How could her mother be so completely insensitive? She had lots of people to call: Trig, Bernadette, Aunt Ivy, Grandma, KIRO TV's recorded weather report, the Orlando Bloom fan-club hotline. She was about to rattle off her complete list to prove she had a life when her mother held out a pink envelope. "Card for you."

"Me?" Easter was over, and her birthday was more than two months away.

Momentarily putting Operation Cell Phone on hold, Julep plucked the envelope from her mom's hand. Tucking her thumb under the flap, she ripped it open and slid out the card. On the front was a photograph of a plump, brown sparrow perched on holly branch. Under the picture, it said: *A Pet Is Forever.*

Uh-oh.

Julep tried to keep her hand steady and her face blank as she opened the card:

> *Dear Julep:*
>
> *I was so sorry to hear about the loss of your parakeet. Music can be a great comfort during sad times like these. Hope you are feeling well enough to play again soon.*
>
> *Warmest Wishes,*
>
> *Frieda Pahtoshnik*

"Parakeet?" Her mother was reading over her shoulder. "What's this? Look at this, Bill, Frieda Pahtoshnik sent Julep the oddest card."

Creeping backward to the family room, Julep let out a shrill laugh. "It must be a mistake. I can't imagine where she got the idea that we had a bird, especially a dead one. Ha, ha . . . ha. I'll tell her she was mistaken at my lesson next week. She'll really get a laugh out of that. In fact, I was just about to go practice my scales . . . ha . . . ha . . ."

"Julep Antoinette O'Toole. Hold it, right there."

Julep knew the best thing to do was calmly admit what she (and Trig) had done to break her out of piano prison. The right thing to do would be to own up to everything, gracefully endure her punishment, and accept her destiny: piano lessons every Monday afternoon for the rest of her life. The right thing would have made her parents happy. It would, however, have made her miserable. Julep knew she had to do something to save herself, and she had to do it now.

"I hate the piano," burst Julep. "I hate everything about it. I hate playing scales. I hate practicing. And I hate recitals." She was really on a roll now. "I hate that awful metronome. I hate having frozen fingers all the time. I hate—"

"Just a minute here—" Her mom tried to cut her off.

"No!" Julep shouted, the sharp crack of her voice surprising even herself. "I'm tired of doing things your way all the time. What about my way? Why can't I have a way? I like meat, Mom. Do you even know that about me? I *like* hamburgers and hot dogs and steak. I hate squash. I hate broccoli." She pointed at the casserole on the counter and growled. "I especially hate them together."

Her mother was shaking her head. "You don't mean—"

"I *do* mean!" She slapped her hand on the edge of the

counter. "What I hate most of all is that nobody cares. Nobody ever bothers to ask what I like and what I don't like. I'm not a baby anymore. If I want to wear an S.E. tee or have a cell phone or quit piano"—she had to pause to gulp back her tears—"then why can't I? Why can't I count for something? I'm not a baby. When will you let me grow up?"

Overwhelmed by her emotions and not wanting her parents to see her bawl like the infant she'd just insisted she wasn't, Julep charged for the back door. She flung it open, pushed through the screen door, and took off. Skidding down the rain-slick steps in her fuzzy, lavender bunny slippers, Julep nearly toppled into the escalonia hedge.

Don't you dare fall. Don't you dare give her a reason to laugh at you again.

Flailing her arms, Julep somehow managed to right herself. As she flew down the overgrown path that led to the woods behind their house, she could hear her father calling her name. Yet Julep kept going, stumbling over twigs and spiky rocks and knobby clumps of dirt. Driven by strong winds, big raindrops hit her sideways and soaked into her cotton shirt. Tall, wet grasses and cattails whipped her in the face. When a nettle bush reached out to grab her, Julep fought it off and kept running.

When you are desperate to be free, you do everything and anything to make it happen. You run until your legs feel like they are going to snap. You run until your lungs scream for air. You run as if your very life depends on it.

Because, sometimes, it does.

8 Unspoken Things

Julep trudged up the porch steps, wiping away the rain that dripped from her bangs into her eyes. With each step, her bunny slippers squeaked and pumped out another splish of muddy water. Now completely drenched, her shirt and jeans made her feel as if she'd gained fifty pounds in less than an hour.

Julep's feet were ice. Her head pounded from crying. And her left palm was throbbing. Her stomach was gurgling so loudly that even a steaming heap of squaccoli didn't sound so bad at the moment. She fell against a post on the porch. Julep knew she was going to have to go inside and say she was sorry when she really wasn't. Well, she *was* sorry for yelling, but she wasn't sorry for feeling the way she did.

Her mother opened the back door to hand Julep a blue bath towel. "Leave your slippers outside and come on in."

Julep toweled herself off and placed her lavender bunny slippers next to her mom's wet hiking boots. In the kitchen she saw her favorite robe, the one with the cows in tutus, draped across a dining-room chair.

"Where is everybody?" Julep's voice was hoarse.

"Your dad's gone to his night class. Harmony's at Marielle's working on a history project. Cooper is still fighting off his cold. He's asleep on the couch."

Julep's heart fell. Might as well paint some purple violets on her face because she was about as noticed as the kitchen wallpaper. No one even had taken time out of his/her busy schedule to worry about her whereabouts while she was out in the woods battling the storm of the century.

Her mother went into the family room, leaving her alone to change. Julep stripped off her sopping clothes and slipped into the warmth of her fleece robe. Wrapping her hair in the towel, she swept it up into a turban on top of her head. She scooped up her clothes and put them on top of the washing machine. Barefoot, Julep padded back into the kitchen, which was dark except for the glow of the little light above the stove. She flopped into one of the dining-room chairs to await her mother's return, along with the lecture and punishment that were sure to come.

When her mom walked back into the kitchen, she asked Julep if she wanted something to eat.

"Okay."

"How about hot chocolate and a P, B, and J?"

Julep did a double take, and a cramp ripped through her neck.

You're asking me? You never ask me what I want to eat.

"Yes," she said, trying to shake off the pain.

As her mother prepared the food, neither of them spoke. But it wasn't one of those "you're in big trouble" silences Julep was used to. This silence was different. It was sort of sad, though she couldn't say why it felt that way. It just did.

Her mother brought her a mug of hot chocolate and her sandwich. She sat down in the chair next to Julep and cradled her chin in her hands. Julep noticed a V-shaped wet spot on the front of her heather-gray sweater. It looked like she had washed her face and spilled water on herself. A squiggle of nonwaterproof eyeliner ran down the corner of one eye, and her mother's usually perfect mascara was smeared. With each blink, the tips of her mom's clumpy eyelashes made little black dots on her eyelids. Julep figured her mother had probably been crying, too, over her misbehaving, disrespectful middle child.

Her mother watched Julep eat half of her sandwich before she said, "You don't have to take the piano anymore."

Translation: Go ahead—break your mother's heart.

Nibbling on the crust of her sandwich, Julep nodded. She didn't know what to say. It wasn't that she didn't want the lessons—okay, maybe it was—but it was so much more than that. Julep wanted to be able to choose an instrument to play on her own, instead of having one chosen for her. She wanted someone to ask her opinion, and then value it. She wanted, more than anything, to matter.

"Dead parakeet." Her mom chuckled, pushing a damp lock of hair behind her ear. "I'd like to hear that story."

"It was Trig's idea," Julep muttered between bites. She told her mother about the phone call they'd made to Mrs. P. at school. She ended with, "It's not Trig's fault. I told him to do it. I should take the blame."

"And you will," her mother said. "Your dad and I will discuss your punishment and let you know what we've decided."

Julep bobbed her head. She was too scared to ask if they were going to keep her from going to Aunt Ivy's for spring break. If she couldn't go to Cloud Nine to see her aunt and her beloved alpacas then she did not want to know tonight.

"You *will* have to tell Mrs. Pahtoshnik the truth, though."

"I know." Julep felt guilty for ditching Mrs. P., who certainly didn't deserve it. Mrs. P. never yelled during their lessons, no matter how many mistakes Julep made (and she made a lot). She even had a snack on hand, usually oatmeal cookies or apple chips, so Julep wouldn't get too hungry before dinner.

Julep wrapped her palm around the warm mug, and pain shot through her hand. She cried out, nearly spilling her cocoa all over the table and herself.

"What is it?"

"I've got a splinter or nettle in my hand." Julep tried to inspect it in the dim light, but couldn't see anything. However, she could certainly feel it. Why was it that the tiniest stickers always hurt the worst?

"Get the tweezers from the first-aid kit," instructed her mother, sliding out of her chair. "Then soak your hand in warm

96

water for a few minutes. While you do that I'll go put Coop to bed. Once your hand is ready, we'll get that splinter out."

Julep shrank back. "It's okay, you don't have to—"

"You don't want an infection."

"It's going to hurt."

"It'll be all right."

"But, Mom—"

"Just for once, Julep, can't you . . ." Her mother stopped at the doorway. For a second, it seemed like she was going to turn around and finish her thought, but instead, she kept going.

That was their problem, Julep felt: the unspoken things. The things they couldn't, or wouldn't, talk about with each other. Julep didn't know why it was so hard for the two of them to communicate. Maybe they were afraid of what the other would say. Or maybe it was simpler than that. Maybe they both didn't know how to start. Since neither of them ever took the chance, nothing important ever got said.

In the laundry room, Julep found the tweezers in the first-aid kit. As she slid the box back onto the shelf, her arm brushed against something wet. It was the sleeve of her mother's navy Lands' End jacket; the goose-down one she wore whenever they went camping. Except, they hadn't been camping since their trip to Mount Rainier last month.

Weird.

With her hand stuck in a bowl of warm water, Julep kept thinking about her mom's jacket. The more she thought about it, the more everything began to fall into place. A wet, navy parka in the laundry room. Muddy hiking boots on the porch. Streaked mascara. Damp hair. A water spot on the front of her mom's heather-gray sweater.

Could it be?

No.

Would *she,* of all people, have—?

Maybe.

When Julep had bolted out of the house, it seemed as if everyone had forgotten her the moment the door had slammed shut behind her. After all, her dad had left for his class. Harmony had gone to Marielle's. Cooper had gone to sleep. No one had worried about her, or cared enough to come after her. Or had they?

Suppose someone had put on her goose-down parka and hiking boots. Suppose someone had followed Julep down to the pond, staying close enough to make sure she was safe but remaining far enough away to allow her some privacy to think. And cry. Suppose it was the same person who was holding her hand right now, carefully digging out a stubborn thorn.

What then?

Feeling a slight pressure on her palm, Julep shifted her gaze upward and tried not to stiffen. She braced herself, waiting for the sting that was sure to come.

"It's out."

Julep glanced down to see barely a sliver of a nettle clinging to the tip of the tweezers. She'd barely felt a thing.

In the O'Toole family, there were three basic types of grounding. Harmony had coined the names, having been the first child to experience each type of punishment. First and lowest on the scale was "takeaways." This level usually involved small infractions, such as arguing with a sibling, forgetting to do a chore, or not getting home from a friend's house on time. Phone, computer, stereo, television, and/or social privileges could be "taken away" for a few hours up to several days, depending on the severity of the crime and the mood of the particular parent passing sentence.

Next was "minor grounding," which covered such things as incomplete homework assignments, not doing something you were asked to do at least twice (or doing something you were asked to do so poorly that a parent had to do it over again), and pretty much anytime a teacher called your house. Like all groundings, minor grounding kept you inside and away from friends, but usually allowed you to use essential household equipment (i.e., stereo, TV, computer, and phone), though for short, restricted periods of time. Minor groundings typically lasted no more than two weeks.

Finally, there was the most serious punishment of all: "major grounding." At this highest level, you were trapped inside and all privileges were suspended usually for two weeks or more. No use of household equipment. No friends. No social engagements. No activities. No fun was to be had at any time. In addition, you'd often have extra chores to do, lest you think you were going to get off easy and sleep your way through your sentence.

For skipping her piano lesson and lying to Mrs. Pahtoshnik and her parents, Julep knew the penalty would be stiff. But nothing could have prepared her for what happened the following night when her mother and father called her into the family room.

"Julep, we trusted that you were going to your lesson after school," said her dad. "This is a real disappointment."

"I know," she croaked. "I'm sorry."

It was true. She'd had plenty of time over the last twenty-four hours to weigh her actions, and she realized she'd made a fatal mistake. In skipping the lesson, Julep had thought she was winning the war for her freedom. Instead, she had lost ground. It would be a long time before her parents would put their faith in her again. And even longer, she feared, before they would give her any space to be herself. They would be watching her every move now—where she went, what she did, and when she did it. She might never get to choose anything for herself ever again.

"How often have you been skipping piano?" asked her mother.

"This is the first time." She crossed her heart. "I promise."

"We want to believe you."

Julep stared at her feet. She didn't blame them for being skeptical. But what could she say to prove that she was trustworthy? All she could do was give them her sorry face. That was where she lifted her eyebrows, widened her golden-brown eyes, and stuck out her lower lip. At her sister's suggestion, she had also put her hair into pigtails to appear as innocent as possible for her sentencing. But with two knobs of hair sticking out of each side of her head, Julep didn't feel innocent. She felt ridiculous. Here she was demanding to be treated like a grown-up, and she was looking like she belonged in preschool.

She would have to remember to stop taking advice from Harmony.

"You are grounded for a month," said her father. "There will be no use of the TV, phone, or stereo. You can use the computer, but only for homework. You're to come straight home after school. No extracurricular activities or visits from Trig or Bernadette."

Ouch!

Julep had gotten hit with the toughest category: major grounding.

"Your mom and I will make a list of things for you to do each day when you get home from school. We expect *you* to do them." He was referring to the time Julep had sneaked around this rule by paying Cooper a quarter for each of her chores he completed. "Understood?"

"Yes." She wiped her watery eyes and turned to leave.

"We're not done," said her mother.

Julep's neck suddenly felt too weak to support her head. She knew what was coming and wanted to clamp her hands over her ears so she wouldn't have to hear it, but her pigtails were in the way.

"About your trip to Cloud Nine . . ."

A burning sensation tore through Julep's chest. A torrent of hiccuping sobs took over her body. The thought of spending spring vacation with Aunt Ivy and the alpacas she adored so much was the only thing that had been keeping her alive, and now her parents were about to tell her . . .

"Your grounding will be lifted for five days."

Julep's head snapped up. As she gasped for air, she searched their faces. They weren't kidding, were they? They wouldn't tease her about something so important. "I can really . . . I can really . . . ?" She could not seem to say the word *go.*

"You can go," her mom said, nodding.

"But why . . . I mean, I thought . . ."

"It didn't seem right to take away what little time the two of you get to spend together. I couldn't . . . I mean, we couldn't . . . well, your aunt loves you so much."

Brushing away her tears, Julep asked if she could call Bernadette to tell her the trip was on. Her father gave the prisoner permission to make one last phone call.

"I'm going to Cloud Nine!" Julep shouted. She bounded across the family room in two leaps and skidded into the kitchen to get the phone.

Julep's mother let out a soft sigh. "Miss you already," she said in a whisper so thin that nobody heard her, least of all her whirling, twirling, utterly blissful eleven-year-old daughter.

9 JULEP'S TULIP

8:01 P.M.   Mood: Excited!

Dear J:

I am packing for my trip to Cloud Nine. Don't worry, you're at the top of the list. See?

STUFF TO TAKE:

journal	camera
shirts	old pair of gloves (for carrying hay—it itches)
sweaters	jeans
5 pairs of socks	5 pairs of underwear
brush	mousse/styling gel/shampoo
toothbrush	toothpaste
~~blow dryer~~	"Take it and die" (a direct quote from Harmony when she saw me winding up the cord). I prefer to leave it and live.

Aunt Ivy is picking me up at ten o'clock tomorrow, and then we'll swing by to get Bernadette. My mom came in a little while ago (she has an early conference call at work so will be gone when I get up

in the morning). It went okay, the good-bye part, I mean. She said
for me to have fun. I said I would. She said not to forget my
toothbrush. I said I wouldn't. That was about it.

I can hear Cooper. He is having a fit because he wants to go to
Cloud Nine, too. Dad is trying to calm him. With his allergies and
asthma, Coop can't go to my aunt's farm. He has never met any of
the alpacas. It's so sad.

Freedom is just around the corner. Oh, hurry up, tomorrow. HURRY!
                    C.Y.L.,
                    Julep

P.S. I just had an idea. I could put the pictures I take into a
little album and give them to Cooper. That might cheer him up.
Boy, can he wail!

P.P.S. Aunt Ivy named the new <u>cría</u> Amelia! Little Amelia, here
I come!

As the Douglas firs whizzed past at sixty-four miles per hour,
Julep let her eye muscles relax. The towering trees went out of
focus, fading into an endless ribbon of emerald green. For a
while she counted the white mileposts, knowing that with each
passing marker they were 5,280 feet closer to Cloud Nine

Ranch. Soon the hypnotic rhythm of the trees and posts, along with the hum of the car's engine, lulled her to sleep.

When Julep opened her eyes again, they were no longer traveling down Interstate 5. Her aunt's silver SUV was now heading west through the fertile farmlands of the Skagit Valley. This was tulip country. Field after field of flowers bloomed full under the spring sunshine, creating an endless patchwork quilt. As they neared the tiny town of La Conner, traffic slowed to a crawl. People were hanging out their car windows to snap photos of the colorful fields.

"Tourists." Aunt Ivy shook her head at the driver ahead of them, who kept swerving onto the shoulder of the road. "You'd think they'd never seen a flower before."

"Just not so many in one place," said Julep, tapping her friend's arm to wake her up.

Bernadette twitched. "Are we there?"

"Not yet. But look. Wake up and look."

Yawning, Bernadette sat up and stretched. Wiping the sleep from her eyes, she glanced out the car window. "Wow," she said as they passed row after row after row of bright pink tulips. About a half mile up the road, the pink tulips turned bright yellow to form another block in the floral quilt.

"Can we stop? Can we walk down the rows? Can we buy some tulips?" the girls begged.

"All right," said Aunt Ivy, running a hand through her short crop of ash-blond hair. "It's not like we're exactly making great time anyway." She pulled off the road and into a gravel parking lot. The SUV bounced in and out of some deep potholes before coming to rest under a sign that read TIPPI'S TULIPS. Bernadette and Julep scrambled out of the car. Julep forgot her camera and had to go back for it. She slung the leather strap around her neck so it wouldn't fall into the mud.

"Wait!" called her aunt as the girls raced toward the field of yellow tulips. "What color of tulips do you want?"

They stopped short.

Bernadette looked at Julep. Julep looked at Bernadette.

"Purple," they yelled in unison.

"Don't go far."

"We won't," they shouted together, laughing at their synchronicity.

While Aunt Ivy went to the flower stand, Julep and Bernadette each chose a different row to skip down, though they quickly discovered that any type of hopping was virtually impossible. The quicksandlike mud kept trying to suck their shoes off.

"Bern!" Julep called to her friend three rows away. "Crouch down until your face is barely above the tulips so I can take your picture."

Bernadette squatted to line her face up with a clump of yellow blooms. The light wind pushed the stems to the right, making the flowers look like members of a choir all straining to reach the same high note. Bernadette's long, brown hair was flowing with them.

Julep clicked the shutter. "Got it."

The girls continued ambling along their respective rows, occasionally pausing to touch a silky, gold-dipped petal or watch a bee spread pollen. In the distance, Julep noticed an old white barn rising up from the blanket of flowers. Faded, green shingles barely clung to the sloping roof, threatening to break free with the next gust of wind. Above the barn, chunky, cotton-ball clouds somersaulted across the sky. Raising her camera, Julep took a picture of the barn and surrounding fields. This, she decided, would be the first picture in Cooper's photo album.

Bernadette was calling to her. "What is that?"

"Where?"

She pointed west. "That red thing."

Squinting against the sun, Julep struggled to make out the red dot that was at least twenty rows away. "Don't know."

"Race you!"

Each one eager to be the first one to solve the mystery, the girls hurried diagonally through the field. Julep was careful not to step on any delicate leaves or stems, so she was the last to arrive. By the time she got there, Bernadette had already made the discovery. She swung her arm out wide. "How do you suppose this one little guy got stuck all the way out here?"

Catching her breath, Julep could only shake her head in wonder at the single flame-red tulip growing smack in the middle of thousands and thousand and thousands of yellow ones.

"I'll bet you can see it from a mile away," said Bernadette.

"It sure catches your attention," agreed Julep, peering into the middle of the petals to see a splash of yellow in the center.

"Speaking of attention, I think your aunt is trying to get ours."

Aunt Ivy was at the edge of the parking lot, waving an arm over her head.

"Coming!" Julep shouted, falling into step behind Bernadette.

They hadn't gotten very far down the row when Julep paused. She turned around to look at the red tulip one last time. It was a bit taller than the yellow ones. Was it her imagination or did it seem almost happy to be the only stroke of red in a sea of gold?

For the third time that day, Julep raised her camera.

And the red tulip bowed.

10 On Cloud Nine

We're here. We're here!" Julep bounced in her seat as the SUV rolled under a stone archway. Attached to the arch was a wooden sign with the words CLOUD NINE painted in blue and white. At first, the car wound up a steep, forested driveway, but soon the thicket of fir trees parted to reveal a sprawling meadow. White fences divided the rolling, green hills into pastures. As they drove past the duck pond and the new barn, Bernadette was intently peering out the window. Julep could tell her friend was searching for one of the strange animals she'd heard so much about. Yet they didn't see so much as a goat.

Julep merely smiled knowingly.

Aunt Ivy braked next to a light yellow farmhouse with a wraparound wooden porch. Above the kitchen window, rooster wind chimes clinked in the wind. Before Aunt Ivy could unfasten her seat belt, Julep had already flung open her door. She was halfway out when the black-and-white Australian shepherd bolted up to greet her with an exuberant "Arf. Arf, arf."

"Hey, Roscoe." Julep threw her arms around his neck. A

pink, slobbery tongue swept over the entire side of her face. Laughing, she wiped the dog drool from her cheek. "I've missed you, too. Aunt Ivy, is it okay if we—?"

"You know where they are."

"Thanks, Aunt Ivy. I love you."

"I think you love my alpacas more." Her aunt's crooked grin teased.

Julep latched on to Bernadette's arm to lead her around down the cobblestone path toward the barn. "Remember, no sudden moves. They're easily scared."

"Don't worry," remarked Bernadette. "I'm not getting within spitting range of them."

Rounding the barn, Julep spotted Wisteria first. The cream-colored alpaca was nibbling on a clump of Kentucky bluegrass just on the other side of the fence. The other two females were about twenty yards or so off in the meadow. Cassiopeia and Fancy were nose to nose on a mound as if in the middle of a very important conference. The toasty-brown legs of Amelia, the new *cría*, were barely visible behind her dark brown mother, Fancy. When Bernadette and Julep approached, Wisteria cautiously lifted a woolly, ivory neck. Black saucer eyes with white eyelashes locked on to them. A pair of erect, arrowhead-shaped ears went back, and a nose began to sniff the air.

"He's so cute," gushed Bernadette.

"Actually, he's a she. That's Wisteria. All of the alpacas in this pasture are females. The males are over there." Julep gestured to the south pasture, where Starburst and Sky Dancer were playfully shoving each other.

"You never told me they were so adorable," cried Bernadette, trotting toward Wisteria. "Like a cross between a sheep and a deer. Come here, little lapaca."

"It's *al*paca, and I wouldn't do that," said Julep. "You're going to . . ."

Seeing Bernadette jog toward her with outstretched arms, Wisteria quickly straightened to her full height of about four feet. Raising her white bobbed tail, she let out a low bleat and galloped across the pasture to warn the rest of the herd that something was up.

". . . frighten her," Julep finished.

Hadn't Bernadette heard a thing she'd said?

Bernadette stopped and dropped her arms. "What'd I do wrong?"

"Follow me," said Julep, heading into the barn. She filled the pockets of her windbreaker with a few handfuls of grain. "Alpacas are shy," she explained, motioning for Bernadette to come over so she could put some grain into her pockets, too. "Alpacas are a lot like cats, personality-wise. You have to give them time to get to know you. Once they trust you, they'll let you feed and pet them." Julep enunciated the next three words so her friend would not make the same mistake twice. "No sudden moves."

"Right."

This time, the girls padded in slow motion toward the females grazing on the grassy mound. They kept their arms down and did not speak. Soon three inquisitive heads turned, and dark eyes gazed in their direction with wary suspicion. But nobody ran.

"There's Amelia," whispered Julep, nodding toward the butterscotch ball of fuzz standing under Fancy, suckling milk. The *cría* was a month old, but was small for her age because she had been born three weeks early (she weighed barely ten pounds at birth). Sometimes, a *cría* would have to get on its knees to nurse from its mother, but not Amelia. She had to lift her head. After a few more minutes, Amelia appeared out from under Fancy's dark belly. A thin neck stretched upward. At her full height, she was barely three feet tall. Her small head just reached her mother's front shoulders. Amelia's ears, however, looked like they'd been growing at twice the rate as the rest of her body.

On long, thin legs, Amelia toddled around Bernadette and Julep. She circled them twice and seemed to want to venture closer. Yet when Bernadette extended her hand, the *cría* immediately zipped back to her mother.

"She's wonderful," said Bernadette. "Knobby knees, eyelashes, and all."

It took a while of simply standing and waiting awhile (a loooooong while), but eventually Wisteria sidled up to Julep. Julep held still while a wet nose sniffed her neck and ears, which wasn't easy because it meant squelching the automatic giggles that come when you're tickled in a sensitive area. With Wisteria nuzzling her, Julep put out her arm to touch the lush fleece of her neck. She never tired of stroking the velvety fluffs of crimped fur.

"What's that noise?" Bernadette leaned in. "It sounds like squeaky wagon wheels."

"That's Cassiopeia. She's talking to you. It's called humming."

"What is she saying?"

"Who are you? What do you want? Can I have some grain?" Julep delicately petted Wisteria's topknot, the puffy, white tuft of fur on her forehead. Wisteria's nose had rooted out the grain in Julep's pocket. Julep brought out a handful and held it out for Wisteria to eat.

"I'm Bernadette," Julep heard her friend whisper to the smoky-gray creature that had crept up for a whiff of her hair.

"She has the most amazing fur," said Julep. "Spread her fleece apart."

Bernadette didn't budge.

"She won't bite."

"Are you sure?"

"Absolutely. They only have bottom teeth and a dental pad on top to nip off grass. Some of the males have molars, but they have to be pretty angry to bite. When they do get mad, it's usually at one another not humans."

It took Bernadette a few minutes to get up the nerve to

touch Cassiopeia. "She's so soft," she exclaimed, gently pushing apart the fleece the way Julep had directed to look beneath
the top layer. "Oh, my gosh. It's pink!"

"She's a rose-gray alpaca."

At that moment, Bernadette's pants began to play a tune. A
wary Wisteria scooted backward. Four sets of alpaca ears
twitched with concern as Bernadette fumbled for her cell
phone.

"Hello? Hi, Mom." She lowered her voice. "Yeah, we got
here okay. We're outside with the alpacas right now. We're
feeding them grain. They take it right from your hand. I'm
feeding Cassiopeia. She's what they call a rose-gray al—oh,
sure. Sorry. You go. Uh-huh. Uh-huh . . ."

"Hello, girl," soothed Julep, coaxing Wisteria back to her
with more grain. "I'm so happy to see you."

"I guess so." Bernadette turned away. "I thought we were
going to the zoo together—yeah, but there's the butterfly exhibit—okay. Okay. Whatever."

There was a long pause, followed by Bernadette stubbing
her toe into the ground several times. Obviously, something
was wrong.

Julep wondered if she should let Bernadette have some
privacy.

"I said it was okay, didn't I? I don't care. Get what you want.
Fine. Yeah. Yeah. Bye."

Julep wasn't sure if she should say anything about what
she'd overheard. It might make things worse. She decided the

best thing to do was wait. Bernadette would bring it up if she really wanted to talk about it.

For a long time, the girls remained quiet, content to let the alpacas empty their pockets of grain.

"Bern?"

"Yeah?"

"I have something to tell you."

"What?"

"I can't have a cell phone."

"You can't?"

"My mother said I didn't need one 'cause I had nobody to call. How rude is that? Anyway, I'm sorry we can't take pictures and send them to each other. I should have told you before, but I didn't want you to be mad at me."

Bernadette put her hand on Cassiopeia's side. "It's okay," she said, stroking her.

That was it? After weeks of harassing Julep about how she simply *had* to get a cell phone, all Bernadette could say to this dreadful news was "okay"?

"So are you? Mad, I mean?"

"If you can't have one, you can't have one."

"So not fair. Hey." Julep snickered as an idea filtered into her brain. "You want to trade Moms? Just for a couple of days so I can get a cell phone, some makeup, and a few other important things?"

Bernadette didn't answer. Her head was bent, and her long, dark hair hung in her face.

115

Julep knew it!

"You *are* mad."

Bernadette glanced up and swept her hair back. Behind her gold glasses, her eyes seemed misty. "No," she said, gazing across the peaceful pasture. "I'm not. I don't want to waste a single minute here being mad. Do you?"

Julep grinned.

Already, Bernadette understood.

Cloud Nine was like nowhere else on Earth. This enchanted place had the power to stop time, or at least to slow it. Here, the sun dawdled toward the horizon. The wind waltzed through the prairie grass. Everything moved in rhythm with the simple, docile pace of the alpacas. There was unseen glitter here, unseen magic. If you let down your guard, if you trusted your heart, the sparkle would rub off on you.

Cloud Nine made Julep believe that anything could happen. It made her trust that everything was possible. And always, always, always it filled her spirit to the brim.

8:53 P.M.   Mood: Relaxed

Dear J:

Tonight, Aunt Ivy showed us how to spin alpaca fiber into yarn. She let us try, and it was much harder than it looked. My yarn came out all lumpy and frayed. N.A.P.S.

Time for ALPACA SCHOOL:

- There are two types of alpacas: huacaya (wah—ky—uh) and suri (sir—ee). Aunt Ivy has only huacaya alpacas (S.T.T.T.F!). Ninety—five percent of all alpacas are huacaya.

- Alpacas come in more than twenty different colors. Rose gray and white are my favorites. Bernadette says she likes Fancy's dark brown coloring best. G.C.!

- When an alpaca gets pregnant, it takes 335 days for the cría to be born——that's eleven months!

- Huacaya hair grows in a wavy S shape and fluffs out from their bodies. Suri fleece is long and silky. It hangs down in thin ringlets or dreadlocks.

suri hair   huacaya hair   Julep hair

Harmony is right. I do have alpaca hair.

My mom called. It's only been eight hours since we left home. W.A.N.! Here's an exact transcript of our conversation:

"Did you get there okay?"

"Yeah." (If I hadn't, would I be talking to you right now?)

"Don't forget to wear your coat if it gets chilly."

"I won't." (I never do.)

"Be sure and help your aunt."

"I will." (I always do.)

"Bye."

"Bye."

Gripping, huh? My mom did not say one thing about missing me. Bernadette and I are going to share the big feather bed in the guest room. I'm sleepy from the cheese pizza we made for dinner. It was actual REAL mozzarella cheese, too, not that soy goop my mother buys. So I'll say good night now. Good night now. Ha!

C.Y.L,

Julep

P.S.: *I wonder what Cooper is doing to my shoes!*

Julep's Decoder Page
SHOO FLY!

N.A.P.S.: Not a Pretty Sight

S.T.T.T.F.: Say That Ten Times Fast!

G.C.: Good Choice

SCRAM SPAMHEAD

(that means you!)

11   AMELIA'S COAT

At eighteen minutes to six, Julep opened her eyes. Bernadette was snoring. Again. Julep put her pillow over her head to shut out another series of pig grunts. It didn't work. At twelve minutes to six, she slid out from under the goose-down comforter, stretched, and padded down the hall to the bathroom in her bare feet. After showering, Julep towel-dried her hair and ran a brush through the waves. She put on her favorite pair of faded jeans and her lime-green chenille sweater with the high, button-up collar. As she was pulling on the new white alpaca socks her aunt had knitted for her (Bernadette had gotten a pair, too), she smelled coffee.

Aunt Ivy was up, too.

Popping downstairs and into the burgundy-and-green kitchen, Julep was greeted by dozens of roosters. They cockadoodle-dooed up the wallpaper, pranced over chair cushions, and bobbed across the tile backsplash behind the stove. Aunt Ivy also had rooster baskets, rooster bowls, rooster towels, and rooster oven mitts. She also had a live rooster name Reverb, who was pacing out on the back porch. Reverb peered through the window as if he were more than a little put out that all of the fake roosters got to live in the house while he was stuck outside.

"Morning." Julep carefully stepped over Roscoe, who was napping on—what else—an oval rooster rug.

Aunt Ivy turned from the window, the steam from her cup of coffee leaving a circle of fog on the glass.

"Morning," she said with a smile that reminded Julep of her own mother. They were sisters, after all, though Ivy was three years younger. Both were tall and slim, with slightly off-center grins and a sprinkle of freckles across their noses (Julep knew exactly which side of the family to blame for *her* eighty-seven face freckles). Her mother and aunt may have looked alike, but their personalities were totally different.

Julep's mom had a set routine. She never took any chances, never did anything that wasn't carefully planned out. Not even when it came to food. Monday was veggie-burger night. Tuesday was squaccoli night. The only drama came on Friday night when she had to decide between cabbage or seaweed soup.

Two words: yawn fest.

Aunt Ivy, in contrast, was always up for a new adventure at the spur of the moment. Before buying the alpaca ranch, she had been a wildlife photographer. Ivy Gallardo was used to traveling across the globe at a moment's notice. She'd send Julep postcards from strange and wonderful cities like Kuala Lumpur, Fortaleza, and Toamasina—places that Julep had never even heard of. Before tacking the postcard to her bulletin board, Julep would spin her globe until, at last, she found these locations in Malaysia, Brazil, and Madagascar. Julep knew one thing for certain: She wanted to grow up to be exactly like her aunt. She longed to explore the unexplored and discover incredible things about the world and herself. You couldn't test your limits if you were worried about Tuesday being squaccoli night.

"You're up early," said Aunt Ivy.

"Bernadette snores."

"Did you try turning her on her side?"

"Yep."

"And?"

"She snores louder." Watching her aunt's rooster prance around the porch, Julep frowned. "The sun's coming up. How come Reverb didn't wake us?"

"The vet says he has a sore throat. Personally, I think he's faking it for attention."

"Sounds like Trig." Julep giggled to herself. She poured herself a glass of orange juice.

She loved that first swallow of juice in the morning; the way the cool liquid slides over your tongue, down your throat, and splashes into your empty tummy. Ahhh!

"I thought I'd feed the critters before breakfast," said Aunt Ivy, putting her coffee cup in the sink. "Unless you're hungry now."

"I'm not hungry. I'll help you."

"That's what I like, a willing worker."

"It's not work to me," said Julep, draining the last of her juice. Okay, maybe scooping the piles of alpaca poo *was* work, but Julep didn't mind.

"Foggy and a bit frosty this morning," remarked Aunt Ivy on their way out to the barn. "Let's get Amelia into a *cría* coat."

"I'll d-do it," stammered Julep, the crisp air making her teeth chatter. She was beginning to regret having let her hair dry naturally.

While Aunt Ivy went to fill the trough outside with grain for the females, Julep remained inside the barn. She opened the bottom drawer of the storage cabinet and pawed through several *cría* coats. The thick squares of fleecy blanket material had Velcro tabs sewn in and were designed to give the little ones, like Amelia, a bit of extra warmth around the midsection on chilly days. The trick was going to be convincing the quick-footed fluffball of energy to stand still long enough to slip the thing on. Julep chose a bright red coat that would go nicely with Amelia's toasty fur.

"Do you need some help getting her into it?" called her aunt.

"I can do it," Julep said with more confidence than she felt.

"I'll be at the paddock feeding the boys."

"Okay."

Once her aunt was gone, Julep peered around the stacks of hay to spy on Amelia. The *cría* was standing outside, close to the barn door. She seemed to be trying to decide if she wanted to stay with her mother, who was eating breakfast, or venture out into the pasture by herself. As gently and quietly as possible, Julep crept toward her.

When the baby alpaca saw Julep approach, she wiggled her ears and cocked her head. Julep inched a bit closer. Amelia skirted away. Julep tried again, and Amelia shot out of reach. If Julep went right, Amelia dodged left, and vice versa. Just when Julep thought the *cría* might stay put for more than five seconds, four long legs skittered away to do mini–figure eights around her.

"Amelia," groaned Julep, after losing several rounds of catch-me-if-you-can. "You're supposed to wear this. Please be a good girl and come here. It's for your own good."

A pair of playful, black eyes blinked at her.

No matter what Julep did, or how carefully she did it, Amelia refused to let her come near.

"You're impossible," Julep said, watching the *cría* skip off again.

Defeated, Julep went back into the barn and sat down on a bale of hay to await her aunt's return. Between the two of them, they would be able to hold Amelia long enough to get the coat on.

Barely five minutes had passed when Julep felt a tug on her jacket. A nose was probing the back of her jeans. Ever so slowly, Julep lifted the fleece square from her lap and placed it over Amelia's back. The *cría* raised her neck, but did not sprint away. Holding her breath, Julep spread the coat over Amelia's shoulders, fastening the Velcro strips in front. She wasted no time sliding a hand under her belly to attach the strips underneath. In a few seconds, it was all over. She had done it. She had gotten Amelia into her red coat.

"Whew!" Julep said triumphantly, wiping her forehead.

Amelia scampered back to her mother to begin nursing.

"Good job." Aunt Ivy came into the barn and tossed her empty bucket aside. "She likes to make a game of it, you know."

"You could have told me that."

"And spoil her fun? Ready to scoop poo?"

Julep held her nose and said, in a nasal tone, "Sure."

Aunt Ivy went for the wheelbarrow. Julep got a couple of shovels from the corner.

"Did I miss anything?" Bernadette stood in the doorway.

"Nope." Julep held out a shovel for her. "You're right on time."

A little while later, Julep was spreading hay along the ground in the ladies' pasture when she noticed something weird. About thirty yards off, Fancy was nudging Amelia toward the fence. The mother alpaca was nipping at her *cría*'s chest. Amelia was moving from side to side, trying to get around her mother, but Fancy was determined not to let her go.

Julep called for her aunt, then watched as Fancy nipped her daughter once more—this time on the shoulder. Amelia twisted her neck and scooted back against the fence. She had nowhere to go. She was frightened.

"Aunt Ivy!" Julep screeched as loudly as she could.

Her aunt jogged out of the barn, wearing her brown, suede work gloves.

"It's Fancy," gasped Julep. "I . . . I think she's mad at Amelia. She's trying to hurt her."

Aunt Ivy looked toward where Julep was frantically pointing. "What the . . . ?"

The two of them rushed across the pasture. As they got closer, Julep could see that the belly strap on the *cría* coat had come undone. The red fleece cover was flapping loose on Amelia's back. Fancy leaned forward, snapping at her baby again. When Julep started to run to protect the *cría*, Aunt Ivy put out an arm to catch her niece. "Wait."

Julep was crying now. "But we have to stop her. She's going to hurt—"

"Look, Julep. Look." Ivy moved right, pulling Julep with her. From another angle, Julep watched Fancy reach for Amelia again, but from this viewpoint she realized that the three-year-old mother wasn't attacking her *cría* at all. She was aiming for the fleece coat!

Fancy grabbed the material in her mouth and tugged a few more times, until the Velcro tabs in front ripped apart. The red coat slid off Amelia's thin, fuzzy body and fell to the ground. Fancy put one foot on the coat, looked down at it for a moment, and then turned away. Calmly, she followed the fence line out into the meadow, her now coatless *cría* trailing close behind.

"That's a new one." Aunt Ivy shook her head. "I guess Mama doesn't care for red."

A relieved Julep grinned through her tears. "I can't imagine why. I mean, it wasn't like it said HOT GIRL on it or anything."

At that, Aunt Ivy put an arm around her shoulders. "I meant to tell you how sorry I was about that . . . that situation."

"She made me take it back, you know."

"I know."

"You didn't think there was anything wrong with it, did you?"

"That's not the point. *I* am not your mother."

"No," Julep said. "*My* mother freaks out over everything. You should have seen her when Harmony put a teeny dab of blush on my face. She went supersonic. She doesn't think I'm old enough to do anything on my own. She hates me."

"She loves you," countered Aunt Ivy firmly. "You can't see it 'cause you're trapped in the mother–daughter time warp."

"The what?"

"The mother–daughter time warp. You've never heard of it?" Aunt Ivy was teasing her.

"There's no such thing," said Julep.

"Sure there is. Practically every mother and daughter in the world get sucked into it. You're trying to make time go faster so you can grow up. She's trying to slow it down so you'll stick around and be her little girl for a bit longer."

Julep had never thought about it in quite that way before. It did make sense. Kind of. Eventually, though, her mother was going to have to get a grip and realize that nobody could stop time.

"Okay, so we're in the mother–daughter time warp." Julep was willing to play along. "What are we supposed to do about it?"

Spinning to walk backward, Aunt Ivy munched on her lower lip. "I don't know. I guess you both have to reset your clocks so you're in sync."

"And how are we supposed to do that?" asked Julep, rolling her eyes. "We can't even agree on a stupid shirt."

Before disappearing into the barn, her aunt said, "You'll figure it out."

Julep doubted that.

The gap between her mother and her seemed to be expanding every day, practically by the hour. What if they were stuck in the mother–daughter time warp forever? What if they *never* found a way to communicate?

Gazing out over the meadow, Julep caught sight of Amelia and Fancy. The *cría* jumped in front of her mother, lowering her body and spreading her legs wide. With a dip of her head and a mischievous bleat, she dashed away. The game was on. Mother and daughter raced back and forth over the pasture, taking turns chasing and being chased. Julep watched until the romping figures disappeared into the early-morning fog. Julep shuffled to the fence and picked up the red fleece square off the ground. Dusting off bits of hay and Fancy's footprints, she carefully folded the *cría* coat and went into the barn to put it away.

12 To Be Continued on Next Shirt

Y ou awake?" Bernadette's voice broke the stillness.

"Huh-uh," a drowsy Julep heard herself say. She snuggled deeper into the feather bed, pulling the comforter up to her chin.

"I can't believe it's been four days already. I never thought I'd have so much fun without a TV. Thanks for inviting me."

"Uh-huh."

"Julep? If I tell you something, you won't tell Trig, will you?"

There was something in Bernadette's tone that made Julep struggle to open her heavy eyes.

"No," she yawned, peering out from under the covers.

Bernadette was staring up at the ceiling. "You remember what you said, you know, about trading moms?"

Julep rubbed her eye. "I was kidding—"

"See, the thing is . . . my mom, she's not . . . I know you think she's, like, the best mom on the planet and everything." Bernadette glanced at Julep. She looked different without her rectangular glasses on her nose. Bernadette but not Bernadette. "The truth is we don't get along very well."

"You don't?"

"We argue all the time."

"Same here," said Julep. "At least, you get to do whatever you want whenever you want to do it. Your mom trusts you. Plus, you get lots of cool stuff like S.E. tees, makeup, and your camera phone. How bad could it—"

"Why are you defending her? You don't know anything about my life."

Stung by her friend's comment, Julep abruptly turned away.

After a long pause, Bernadette said, "I'm sorry. It's just that everything has changed, since the divorce, I mean. And I'm having a hard time."

Turning back, Julep bent her elbow and lifted her head to rest it on her palm. "Changed? How?"

"My dad's got a new girlfriend, my mom's got a new boyfriend, and suddenly there's no room for me. It's like my parents reconstructed our family, and I ended up being a spare part that nobody needed. I don't know . . . I can buy anything and do anything as long as I don't talk about the divorce. Except, see, that's the thing. The one thing I want *is* to talk about the divorce. I want to figure out where I fit—if I fit in."

"Did you tell your mom and dad?"

"I tried once. I got a new stereo." Bernadette grunted like it was funny, but they both knew it wasn't.

Julep was surprised. Bernadette's parents had gotten divorced more than a year ago. Yet not once in all this time had Bernadette mentioned what she was going through. Some friend Julep was. How could she not have noticed that her co-best friend was miserable? Maybe, like Bernadette's parents, she hadn't wanted to see it. She had wanted Bernadette to be perfectly fine after the divorce, and so Julep had pretended that she was. But pretending didn't make it so.

"When I asked my mother if I could see my dad more often," Bernadette was saying, "I got the camera phone. I guess that's her way of saying that's as close as I'm going to get."

Julep didn't know what to say. She put out a hand to touch Bernadette's shoulder.

"My mom is not going to be there when we get home to-morrow." Bernadette's voice broke. "She's going to Sun Valley with Pablo. That's her new boyfriend. He wears tan pants with black underwear!"

"Noooo."

"Yes!"

They both gagged.

"I have to go to my grandma's," said Bernadette. "But I get a new TV for my room."

"With a DVD player?"

"Naturally," she said flatly. "I should get an S.E. tee that says DOES ANYBODY CARE?"

"S.E. tees are so dumb," blurted Julep.

Immediately she bolted upright in bed.

Did I just say that?

Yes! Yes, she had.

You know what this means, don't you?

Yes, unfortunately she knew.

*You only got one because everybody at school was wearing them.
And guess what?*

Oh, please don't say it.

You're not everybody.

You had to say it, didn't you?

The only thing worse than your mother being right, is your mother being right even when she is a hundred and twenty miles away.

Julep collapsed onto the pillows.

No wonder she had stubbornly refused to take off her thick hand-knit sweater the day of the spelling bee. Deep down, she'd always felt that the HOT GIRL tee was pretty dumb. And deeper still, she hadn't really wanted to defy her mom by wearing something that she didn't even like. That's why she had kept the sweater on. That's why she'd fainted—not because she was like everyone else, but because she wasn't. Maybe Julep was more independent than she'd realized.

"S.E. tees are pretty ridiculous when you think about it," said Bernadette. "Everyone's walking around in shirts that say FABULOUS BABE and BOY BAIT—how stupid is that?"

"How about that one Betsy wears?"

"DAZZLE ME?"

"No, the other one"

"You mean LITTLE ANGEL."

Julep snorted. "There should be a law against lying on an S.E. tee."

"If everybody had to be honest, Danica would have to wear one that said I THINK I'M SO SUPERIOR."

"Or I ONLY WEAR ITALIAN SHOES."

"DID I SAY YOU COULD SIT HERE?"

"I COPY OFF SMITTY'S TEST PAPERS."

"I AM THE SQUARE DANCE QUEEN."

The girls laughed so hard they both got side cramps. They were trying to breathe normally again when the bedroom door squeaked.

"It's almost midnight. Who's giggling in my feather bed?"

Squealing, Julep and Bernadette threw the comforter over their heads.

"Get some rest now, okay? Good night, Giggle Girls."

"Good night," they said in unison.

Still under the covers, Bernadette snickered. "I have one for Betsy. How about COULD MY EARRINGS BE ANY BIGGER?"

"COULD MY EARS?"

Bernadette exploded, and Julep jumped to clamp a hand over her mouth so they wouldn't get in trouble again.

"Hey, Bern," Julep said as they were dozing off, "you can talk to me about divorce stuff anytime you want. Anytime. I'll just listen, okay?"

"Okay."

Julep didn't know why she'd thought S.E. tees were so great in the first place. After all, they weren't really *you* expressing yourself. But what if everybody's true feelings magically appeared across their chest, like some sort of Etch A Sketch S.E.

tee? Wouldn't that be something? No one could pretend to be happy when they were really suffering or calm when they were frightened or content when they were uncomfortable. No one would have to be alone, because there was bound to be someone, somewhere who had a shirt that matched yours. Someone, somewhere in the world would understand. That would sure make it a whole lot easier than trying to guess what was going on in your best friend's heart. And yours, too, for that matter.

Julep imagined what her different shirts might say.

EMBARRASSED TO DEATH ON A DAILY BASIS
MY MOM AND I DON'T EVEN SPEAK THE SAME LANGUAGE
INDEPENDENT GIRL UNDER CONSTRUCTION
TO BE CONTINUED ON NEXT SHIRT . . .

With all of the stuff going on in her life, Julep would definitely need a bigger closet.

Not to mention a bigger chest!

9:23 A.M.   Mood: Quiet

Dear J:
We're leaving Cloud Nine in exactly thirty-seven minutes (sniff, sniff). I'm sitting under the crabapple tree near the pond, watching Mr. and Mrs. Mallard try to round up their fourteen

ducklings and get them into the water. They are all dark brown, except for one yellow one that wants to zoom off in a different direction from the rest. I wonder if her name is Julep.

I will never forget this spring break.
I will never forget Amelia (I have
TONS of photos of her for Cooper).

I will never forget how fun it was to spin
fleece into yarn (even if mine did look
like something Bernadette's cat,
Pounce, upchucked)!

As you know, I've been thinking for a long time about what to name you. Now, at LOOOOONG last, I think I have the perfect name. It has to be special, the way you are special to me. I mean, you know me better than anyone (scary, huh?). You always listen to my feelings, thoughts, and ideas (even the weird ones). When I finish writing, somehow I just know that everything in my crazy life is going to work out all right. Anyway, I want to name you

In midsentence, Julep lifted her pink gel pen from the page.

Chewing on the rounded top, she reread her last paragraph. She was getting an idea.

It might be, she thought, the way to escape the mother-daughter time warp. Of course, it would mean a whole new way of communicating, but perhaps that was exactly what the two of them needed—something new, something different, something totally unexpected.

But would her mom go for it?

Julep didn't know, but she was willing to find out.

Scrambling to her feet, she ran across the meadow. "Sorry, ladies," she called, passing the group of bewildered alpacas on their mound.

Julep never expected that she would want to leave Cloud Nine early, but she had an important stop to make in La Conner. Besides, she would be coming back to this place again very soon. She could feel it in her spirit. She belonged here. Nothing would ever, could ever, keep her away.

Racing toward the house, Julep prayed it wasn't too late to reset their clocks.

This might be their one and only chance to get it right.

13 Independence Day

Dear Mom—

Sometimes it is hard to tell someone what you are feeling, especially when you aren't even sure yourself. It is hard to find the right words. It can be even harder to say them. But I want to try, because . . . well, just because.

No, that's not true. I'm going to be honest. I want to try because I love you.

I bought this book with my allowance. I want it to be our friendship journal. It is just for you and me. Nobody else in the entire world will write in it or be allowed to read it (not even Dad). In here, we can write or draw whatever we want to each other. We can ask questions, share stuff, and tell jokes (Why did the cow cross the road? The answer is at the bottom of the page). When I write in it, I will leave it under your pillow. When you are done making an entry, you can leave it under mine. I hope you will think this is a good idea and want to do it with me.

Your daughter,
Julep Antoinette O'Toole

P.S.: Do you like the cover?
The two butterflies reminded
me of us. We spend a lot of
time fluttering around each other,
but we never seem to land on
the same flower.

A: To get to the udder side, of course!

"Cooper! Let's go. I'm not waiting for you forever."

Leaning on the railing, Julep peered up into the high ceiling above the staircase. A shaft of sunlight had found its way through the circular window at the top and was using the crystal chandelier to paint dozens of tiny, flickering rainbows on the wall.

Julep wondered if her mother had found the journal that she'd tucked under her pillow that morning. Probably not.

Julep had left a good part of the royal-blue corner showing so she would be sure to spot it. But by the way her mother usually darted about, pulling on her panty hose while pouring cereal for Cooper and talking on the phone to Bonnie at work, Julep doubted she would even notice the journal until she laid her head down that night.

That was okay.

Julep could wait. She would be jittery all day, but she could wait.

"*Cooper!*"

"Hold your ponies," his voice boomed from the top of the landing. Trotting down the steps, he wagged a small purple book at her. "I had to get the photo album you made for me. I'm takin' it to school."

Julep beamed. "Oh, for show-and-tell? Your class will love seeing the alpacas—"

"Show-and-tell nothing. Lucas owes me a buck."

Zipping up her windbreaker, she halted midzip. "What do you mean?"

"He didn't believe me when I told him about the alpacas. Now he's gonna have to pay—"

"Cooper." She scowled. "No betting."

"Aw, Jules—"

"Don't make me tell. Do you know you've got a big glob of strawberry jam on your sleeve?"

"I know. I'm saving it for later. Kenny's bringing crackers and we're gonna swap."

"That is the grossest thing—"

"Are we going or not?"

"We're going," she said, shaking her head.

They were only a few minutes late meeting Trig at the corner of Bayview and Chenault. Even so, it had given him plenty of time to turn the Ramplings' IT'S SPRING! daisy flag upside down on its metal pole.

"Fix it," Julep ordered.

Trig was tearing open a snack-size bag of barbecue potato chips with his teeth and pretended he had no clue what she was talking about. Julep put a hand on a hip and glowered at him until, finally, he gave in and put the flag right side up.

"Some criminal you are," muttered Julep, seeing two distinct, barbecue-red fingerprints on the edge of the flag.

"Hey, mini Cooper," teased Trig, holding out the bag of chips. "Want some?"

Cooper was about to dip his fingers into the bag when Julep caught his wrist. "He doesn't, thanks."

Her brother wriggled away. "I do so."

"He does not," she said sternly, trying to wipe strawberry jam off her fingers. "Barbecue potato chips give him a stomachache. Besides, it's not healthy for *anyone* to eat potato chips for breakfast. Now put those away."

"Geez," grumbled Cooper, kicking a pebble. "You sound just like Mom."

"I do not."

"Do so."

"Do not." Julep gave Trig a warning glance to indicate he was not to get involved.

Trig lifted a shoulder as if to say "You kind of do."

"Well, if I do, and I'm not saying I do, it's only 'cause I'm trying to . . ."

They had reached the intersection, and Julep thrust out her hand for her brother to hold on to while they crossed. Cooper took it without pressing her to finish the sentence, which was a huge relief because Julep had been half a heartbeat away from saying . . .

Gulp.

". . . look out for you the best way I know how."

Double gulp.

". . . and then, Mr. Habersetzer gave *me* extra questions to do from Chapter Three, even though Calvin was the one who threw the airplane," Trig said. "Can you believe that?"

"Yeah," said Julep absently, glancing over the top of Bernadette's right shoulder.

She hadn't heard a word Trig had said. Her attention was on something, or rather someone, else. Smitty was at his usual end table. Alone in his invisible workshop, he was brushing a coat of clear varnish on his pyramid, which was now stained a rich walnut brown.

Curiosity tugged at Julep. She was dying to know what it was going to be. What could a person possibly do with a ten-inch pyramid?

"You're only complaining because, for once, you couldn't worm your way out of trouble." Bernadette licked blueberry yogurt off her spoon. She pointed it at Trig, who was sitting to her left. "You did fold the airplane, right?"

"Yeah, but—"

"You did hand it to Calvin to look at, right?"

"Yeah, but—"

"It hit Mr. Habersetzer in the head, right?"

"Yeah, but—and quit interrupting me—I, Trig Maxwell, did NOT throw it."

"Doesn't matter."

"Doesn't matter?"

"You were an accessory to the crime. You do know what that means, don't you?"

"Yeah . . . sure."

"Case closed. Do the questions, Maxwell."

"I wasn't an acc . . . ex . . . whatever you said, was I, Julep? Julep? Where did she go?"

Bernadette checked around. "I don't know. She was just here."

Getting to their feet, the pair squinted toward the ice-cream line, then the pizza line, then finally the garbage cans. But Julep wasn't anywhere in sight.

"She must have gone to the bathroom," concluded Bernadette, sitting back down.

But Julep hadn't gone to the bathroom. If Trig and Bernadette had swung around to look directly behind them, they would have spotted their friend standing by the steps to the stage. Fidgeting with her sleeves and pretending like she was waiting for someone, Julep watched Smitty screw the second of two gold hinges onto the pyramid about a third of the way down from the top.

He looked up at her. She quickly looked away. Smitty went back to work.

Julep edged closer to the table. It took her a few more minutes to gather up the courage to ask, "Is that going to be a robot?"

Smitty glanced up again and looked around to be sure she was talking to him. When he realized she was, he said, "No."

"Oh, well then."

Julep stepped back and was about to leave when Smitty said, "It's nearly done. You want to see it?"

She nodded.

Folding her leg under her, Julep sat down at the table across from Smitty. He set his creation in front of her and lifted open the top section of the pyramid. The lid swung back on its hinges to reveal two wooden doves perched side by side on a tree branch. From somewhere inside, little chimes began to play "Somewhere in Time."

"It's a music box," said Smitty proudly. "A music pyramid, actually."

"Did you carve the doves, too?"

"Yeah," he said shyly. "Be careful," he added when she reached out to touch one smooth side of the pyramid. "The varnish isn't dry yet. It's for my mom, for Mother's Day. You think she'll like it?"

"Sure. Who wouldn't?"

"I hope so," he said. "It's taken me a month to make it."

"I know . . . I mean, yeah," Julep said, becoming aware that the noise level in the cafeteria had suddenly dropped. Was it her imagination, or was everyone in the room staring in their direction? Smitty noticed it, too.

Shifting in his seat, he swung the hinged lid of his music pyramid shut. "The bell's going to ring," he said, putting his tools back in his shoebox.

Out of the corner of her eye, Julep could see the goslings two rows over. Betsy's enormous, gold teardrop earrings twinkled under the fluorescent lights as she held up a piece of notebook paper and looked directly at Julep. The page had a giant *G* on it, written with a pink felt-tip marker. Julep, and everybody else, knew what it stood for: Goser. A few seconds later, Jillian held up an orange *F*.

Julep's eighty-seven freckles felt like they were on fire.

The two girls smashed their papers together and made kissing sounds. People started laughing. Julep had no problem picking out Danica's scratchy laugh above the rest. By now, of course, Bernadette and Trig knew where Julep had gone. They were both motioning like crazy for her to get out of the Goser

Zone and race back to the safety of their table. But it was too late. Julep slipped down in her seat, covering her forehead with her hand.

"You'd . . . I mean I'd . . . I'd better go," said Smitty.

"Yeah," said Julep, shooing him away with the hand that wasn't covering her face.

This was S.N.F. in a big way. Smitty was really, really nice. Okay, he had fashion issues and hair issues. And social issues. And baked-bean issues. But still . . .

The goslings were nothing special. None of them could spell *rancor*, square-dance without injuring their partner, or make a pyramid music box. None of them seemed capable of doing much more than painting their nails when they were supposed to be taking notes in class. So what gave the goslings the right to tell Julep who she could talk to and who she couldn't?

The answer, of course, was simple. Julep had. She had given them that power.

Smitty slid his pyramid onto a sheet of newspaper, tucked his toolbox under his arm, and got up. "See ya."

"Um . . . Smitty, wait." Julep sat up taller and lowered her hand from her face. "You know, today's the last day of our square-dancing unit."

Smitty mumbled that he knew.

"So you . . . you want to be partners again?"

Brushing a long bang out of his eyes, he said, "Sure."

Julep unfolded her leg from beneath her and stood up. "Meet you at the end of the line."

As Smitty walked off, the *swish-swash* of his corduroys could be heard from ten feet away. As usual, the smell of baked beans lingered in the air long after he'd left the building. Some things, Julep knew, might never change. Turning toward the head goose and her goslings, she took a deep bow. But other things, she was certain, would never be the same.

14 Time Travel

Dear Julep:

It was quite a surprise to find this treasure under my pillow! Of course, I want to do a friendship journal with you. What a clever idea. How did you think of it?

I'm looking forward to sharing our thoughts, feelings, and experiences in this book. I can think of nothing better than getting to know you better. Feel free to ask me anything or write about any topic that is on your mind. I promise to keep it top secret (I won't even tell Dad).

I love you,
Mom

Q: What is a mouse's favorite game?
A: Hide-and-squeak.

P.S.: Yes, I really like the butterfly cover! I think it is okay for us to land on different flowers once in a while, as long as we fly together, don't you?

Dear Mom—

Are you serious? ANYTHING? I can really write to you about anything?

Okay, here goes . . .

Can I have a bra? I'd like to get one, and it isn't because Bernadette has one (she doesn't).

You probably think I'm too young, which could be why you made fun of me at the mall when you told the salesgirl that someday I'd be **(fill in the blank)** breasts and we'd be arguing about what kind of bra to buy.

That was why I ran out of the store. I'm sorry I didn't tell you what was the matter when you asked about it. I was just SO embarrassed that you laughed at me. But it's okay now, I'm not mad anymore. I hope you are not, either. Mad, I mean.

So can I? Have a bra, I mean?

Love,
   Julep

P.S.: Are you positive that you are okay with me not taking piano anymore? Be honest. I can take it.

Dear Julep:

Everything is beginning to make sense now. No wonder you were so upset at the mall. I am terribly sorry. I did not think before I spoke to the salesgirl. I should not have said something so personal about you to someone else. Also, you should know that we were not laughing at you. We were giggling because one of the naked mannequins toppled over and landed on her head! Unfortunately, you were in the dressing room and couldn't see that. You must have been so embarrassed to think we were laughing at you. We definitely were not. I love you too much to ever make fun of you!

Next time, when something like this happens, please tell me what is on your mind, okay? That way, we can work it out right there. If I had only known what you were feeling, how differently that day might have turned out.

Yes, you can have a bra. Let's go shopping this weekend (I promise you can pick out whatever one you want, and I won't talk to any salespeople).

I am so proud of you and love you so much (more than Rocky Road ice cream with chocolate sprinkles!).

Yours Always,
Mom

P.S. I am absolutely, positively okay with you not taking piano. Is there some other activity you'd rather do, instead? I just

found your brother's used gum collection under his bed. Please
say you won't do that!

P.P.S.: Write back soon!

"What's that?" Trig inspected the black, rectangular case that Julep was carrying.

"It's a—"

"It's a trumpet," Cooper broke in, kicking his backpack out in front of him.

"I'm joining band," said Julep. "I get to take lessons at Mill Creek Music."

"She's going to need a lot of them," Cooper told Trig. "She sounds like a sick rhino."

"I do not."

"Do so."

"Do not."

Trig nudged Cooper and quipped, "Better get some ear-plugs."

"Already got 'em," said a totally serious Cooper.

When they got to school, Julep headed straight for the band room. Miss Crosetti, the band teacher, assigned Julep a cubby-hole for her trumpet in the instrument storage closet. Miss Crosetti even used her label maker to print out a blue strip that read JULEP O'TOOLE—TRUMPET in white letters. The moment she stuck the label on the shelf, Julep knew it wasn't a dream anymore. Her hope had blossomed into reality. She could not wait to tell Amelia all about it when she got home today. The name seemed to fit her journal, and Julep was certain the real Amelia wouldn't mind sharing her beautiful name with something so special.

"Did you get your schedule rearranged without any problems?" asked Miss Crosetti.

"I have to turn in my signature card this morning to the counselor to switch from chorus to band," said Julep. "But they're the same period, so there's no problem."

"Good." Miss Crosetti smiled at Julep and spoke the words Julep had longed to hear for more than two years, "Welcome to concert band, Julep."

"Thanks."

Julep practically skipped on air the whole way to her locker. Her mind was so busy thinking about her new trumpet it took her four tries to open her locker. Slinging off her backpack, she took out her math book and notebook. Julep also made sure to take her signature card so she could drop it off at the counselor's office before first period. She was getting out of her sweater when Bernadette found her.

"Did you bring your trumpet?"

"It's already in the band room."

"This is going to be the best," squealed her co-best friend. "We get to have another class together—hey, nice shirt. Is that new?"

Julep twirled, modeling the pastel pink, white, and peach

striped shirt. As she spun, she could feel the soft, peach fringe at the hem swaying with her.

Bernadette reached out to touch the heart cutouts going down the sleeve. "This is the one you were telling me about, isn't it? You got it, after all."

"That's not all I got," whispered Julep.

"What do you—"

"I'll tell you later." Julep reached up her shoulder to feel the bra strap under her top.

On their way to the main office, Bernadette and Julep passed Betsy's locker. The head goose and all of the goslings were there, clustered around the open door arguing about whose eye shadow had more sparkle. Out of the corner of her eye, Julep could see four heads swivel to stare at them. She told herself to look straight ahead.

Don't waste even a millisecond on them. They are not worth it.

Yet, despite her promise to ignore the girls, Julep found her head turning their way. And what she saw stopped her cold.

"It's new," said Danica, stepping out of the pack. She flung her long, black hair over one shoulder and put a hand on her waist to strike a pose. "You like it?" she asked Julep in that way people ask when they expect nothing less than the highest of praise.

For the first time in her eleven years on the planet, Julep knew exactly what she wanted to say and how she wanted to say it.

"I might have thought so once," she said, trying to stifle a giggle. "But not anymore."

Julep had found her voice. At last. And it made her feel . . . well . . . free.

With a swish of peach fringe, she left the most popular girl in the sixth grade standing in the middle of the hallway, frowning down at a brand-new, plum spandex tee with the words HOT GIRL scribbled on the chest in glittery gold barrel beads.

It never even crossed Julep's mind to look back.

Turn the page to read
an excerpt from the next book
featuring the lovable Julep O'Toole:

Julep O'Toole

All

I WANT TO DO IS

Direct

1 The Princess and the Pest

Julep, dear, where is your heart?"

Julep glanced down at her black ballet-style shoes, each with a dainty baby-blue heart embroidered on the toe. "Huh?"

The stick figure of a drama teacher scurried toward the cafeteria stage. The heels of her mules went *smick-smack* against the checkerboard tiles. "Emotion, dear. I'm talking about emo-o-o-o-o-tion." When making a point, Mrs. Picklehaupt had a tendency to draw out the second syllable of important words. "Let's try it again. This time, Julep, don't merely read the lines; put some feeling into them. Think about what you're saying. Here is your handsome prince." She threw out a pale, bony arm and her peacock-print scarf slid off one shoulder. "You've waited all your life for him. Look at him. Smile at him. Ado-o-o-o-ore him."

Julep's amber eyes rolled skeptically to the right. Her Prince Charming, the one she'd waited for her entire life, was picking pieces of black licorice out of his teeth. And flicking them at her. Calvin also had a bag of licorice bits stuffed in the pocket of his jeans. Whenever the drama teacher wasn't watching, he'd launch a tiny square at her head. Julep didn't even want to think about how many black cubes were stuck in her kinky mass of reddish-brown hair.

Was Mrs. Picklehaupt completely out of her gourd? With his uneven buzz cut and a mouth dirtier than his ragged fingernails, Calvin Kapinski was nobody's true love. Least of all Julep O'Toole's. He existed only to make each day of her eleven years on Earth as miserable as possible. Calvin was getting so good at tormenting her Julep was pretty sure he was earning credit for it this semester.

"Yeah," said Calvin, waggling a black tongue at her. "Adore me."

"Eat fire ants."

"Now, is that any way to talk to your prince?" Calvin snapped his index finger against his thumb. Julep flinched as a fleck of licorice he'd plucked from between his front teeth landed on the sleeve of her mint-green dragonfly shirt.

"Jerk and a half," she growled, brushing away the goo. It left behind a black streak, which only grew larger when Julep tried to scrub it with a little saliva.

Biting back tears, Julep stared at the floor. She didn't want Calvin or any of the other kids waiting to audition to know how upset she was. She shouldn't even be here trying out for a part in *The Princess and the Pea*. It should never have happened. One minute you're getting a B-minus in second-period English and things are going pretty good. (Well, as good as they get for a middle child whose parents have been known to forget to pick her up from trumpet lessons.) Three quizzes, two essays, and an oral report later, you've dropped to a C-minus. You're so desperate to bring up your grade you'll do anything for extra credit, even agree to be in the school play. Painting scenery was one thing. Having to pretend to be in love with the most disgusting boy in the sixth grade, well . . .

. . . the C-minus was looking better all the time.

It occurred to Julep, as she stood beside a certain pest of a prince armed with edible ammunition, that this was probably how most students got involved in drama—by force. Nobody but an overachiever like Bernadette Reed could possibly consider acting fun. Julep squinted against the row of overhead lights, searching the Heatherwood Middle School cafeteria for any sign of her co-best friend. The honor-society officers meeting had ended ten minutes ago (Bernadette was vice president of the sixth-grade class). Where was she?

Her eyes slowly roving from left to right, Julep finally spotted Bernadette's waist-length mane of dark chocolate hair. Wearing a short jean skirt and a white cotton puckered-front blouse, her friend was sitting at the last table in the first row, though *sitting* was hardly the term for it. Bernadette was bouncing on the bench, tapping the heels of her sandals against the floor, and drumming her fingers on the table. That was the difference between them. Bernadette couldn't wait to get up here, while Julep couldn't wait to escape. Julep had always done her best to avoid things where you couldn't be certain of the outcome. Surprise endings were dangerous. They opened the door for you to humiliate yourself, or worse, be humiliated by someone else.

When their eyes met, Bernadette stopped moving long enough to give Julep a thumbs-up. "Good job," she mouthed, pushing her gold, rectangular, wire-frame glasses up higher on the bridge of her nose.

Julep answered with a feeble wave. Bernadette was sweet, but the pained expressions on the faces of everyone around her told the real story. Julep's acting deserved a big flush down one of the automatic toilets in the girls' bathroom.

Wooooooosh!

Julep *was* trying to do what Mrs. Picklehaupt instructed. But she didn't get it. How was a person supposed to feel things they didn't actually feel, and say things they didn't actually think of? Acting was ridiculous. However, it *was* her only hope of raising her grade in Mr. Lee's English class. And so Julep stayed, doing her best to dodge the hail of black candy that flew her way.

Mrs. Picklehaupt paused to chat with eighth-grader Cherry Anne Oakes, the most famous actress in school. Last year, Cherry Anne had done a television commercial for bug spray. Only one role in *The Princess and the Pea* had already been cast. Cherry Anne was going to be the narrator. The news had come as a surprise. Everyone had assumed Cherry Anne would automatically be chosen for the princess, but a few days ago word had gotten out that Heatherwood's best actress had landed a good part in a *real* play at the Community Playhouse. Someone had overheard Cherry Anne tell Mrs. Picklehaupt that she still wanted to be in the school play, but would prefer a smaller, less demanding part. Translation: the juicy role of the princess was up for grabs. Julep could tell every girl in the cafeteria was drooling after it—every girl but her, of course.

Mrs. Picklehaupt was settling into her chair at the back of the cafeteria. She held up her clear, turquoise clipboard, a signal she was ready for Calvin and Julep to go again. Taking a shallow breath, Julep tried to calm her Jell-O knees. She wasn't good at public speaking, or public anything for that matter. Whenever she had to get up in front of people, Julep's hands began to sweat. Her fingertips went numb. Her eyes had trouble focusing. Her stomach would—

Oh, no! The corn chips she'd gulped down ten minutes ago were doing backflips in her digestive tract. Julep cleared her throat. Calvin let out a long, low burp. Julep took three small steps to the left. Calvin copied her, but took larger steps to close the distance between them.

"Zit Head," she muttered.

"Pooky bear." Calvin made smooching sounds.

Julep gagged, the taste of corn chips coming back to haunt her. She couldn't do this. She could NOT do this.

The sooner you say it, the sooner you can go home and take a boiling hot shower to wash off the Calvin germs.

She could do this.

Julep shielded herself with the script so she wouldn't have to look at *him*. "I know I'm sopping wet from the storm," she said, her voice quivering. "But you must believe me when I tell you that I am far more than I appear. Truly, I am a real . . . I am a real . . . whoa!"

The Princess and the Pea script had leaped from Julep's moist hands. She tried to get it back, but the pair of stapled pages had already caught the breeze from an open window. They fluttered just out of her reach. "One sec," Julep cried. "I'll . . . I'll get it, Mrs. Picklehaupt. Hold on . . ." She tripped across the stage, trying to tune out the snickers coming from the cafeteria. A few feet above Julep's head, her script was happily riding the mini–jet stream. It did several impressive loop-di-loops, giving Julep the chance to scamper across the stage to get ahead of it. Crouching, she waited until the script was directly above her. Then, at the precise moment it came down on the bottom half of a loop, she propelled herself skyward. Julep stretched out her arm, grunted, and grabbed . . . grabbed . . .

Air.

Julep landed on the outside edge of her leather ballet slip-on, rolling her foot under her. Fire shot up the side of her ankle. She collapsed onto the wood floor. Nearing the red velvet curtain at the edge of the stage, the script was losing wind power. It did a slow downward spiral toward the floor. With a groan, Julep got up and limped forward. Gasping, she bent over and snatched up the script. She looked up, barely able to see through a thick cloud of reddish-brown bangs.

Calvin towered over her. "You were saying?"

"Truly I am a . . . a . . ." She tried to catch her breath. "I am a . . ."

"Klutz?" he finished.

The place erupted in laughter.

A rosy glow began to warm the eighty-seven freckles sprinkled over Julep's nose and cheeks. Her right temple began to itch, a sign of her growing anger. Pushing a clump of hair from her eyes, she scrambled to her feet.

"I'm a princess," she shouted, scratching her head. "A prin-CESS. Got it?" Her voice boomed out into the cafeteria. Julep balled up her fists. "And if you think I'm going to sleep on a bunch of old, crusty mattresses to prove it to a toad like you, for-get it." She punched the air only a foot or so from Calvin's face. Calvin's gray coyote eyes doubled in size. His arms snapped up. And two licorice bits fell to the floor.

Fuming, Julep glared out at the audience. One drama teacher and thirty-one middle-school students were gaping at her. Millie Aldridge was madly scouring her script to find where *those* lines were written.

Loud enough for you, Mrs. Picklehaupt? Did it have enough feel-ing? Enough emo-o-o-o-otion? Enough HEART?

It took all of her effort not to say it out loud. Hands on her hips, Julep waited for the criticism that was sure to come. But Mrs. Picklehaupt didn't say a word. Instead, she tossed aside her clipboard and scurried from the auditorium as rapidly as her pointy mules would go.

"Mrs. P.?" called Cherry Anne, hurrying after her.

"I'm going to need a new partner," Calvin tossed into the crowd. Now recovered, he turned to sneer at Julep. "Mine's cracked."

That did it!

Julep threw her script at him. Racing down the front steps of the stage, she sped for the side door of the cafeteria. She felt everybody's eyes on her.

Keep it together. Hold on. You're almost there.

Soon, she would push her way to freedom and fresh air.

Soon, this whole nightmare would be over and she would never again have to do anything so unpredictable. Stupid extra-credit points.

Marching across the tile floor, her arms pumping for maximum speed, Julep realized there was a problem directly ahead of her—four of them actually. Danica Keyes, the most popular girl in the sixth grade, and her tagalong friends, Betsy Foster, Jillian Winters, and Kathleen O'Halleran, had circled their folding chairs in front of the side door. They were blocking her path. Their slouched postures indicated they had no plans to move. When Julep approached, Danica cupped her hands around her mouth. "Ladies and gentleman, Julep O'Toole: fairy-tale princess or professional wrestler? You decide." Her three friends cackled as if it were the most hilarious comment ever made.

Julep did not say a thing. Or make eye contact. However, she did pause long enough to bend forward over their camp and shake her terra-cotta head as hard as she could. A storm of black licorice rained down on the girls. They screamed. But they scattered. Julep kicked past a chair and slammed her body into the door handle. When, at last, she felt the late-afternoon sun on her face, Julep took her first normal breath in an hour. It felt wonderful to fill her lungs. And get the corn chips inside her to quit doing somersaults.

Unlocking her bicycle from the rack behind the gym, Julep felt her shoulders begin to relax. She had to admit the experience wasn't a complete fiasco. The look on Calvin's face after she'd gone bonkers on him was almost worth the humiliation. Almost. In truth, Julep hadn't meant to blow up like that. Her outburst had surprised even her. But Calvin had pushed her too far. He really ought to have known better. Never, never mess with a princess who's having a bad day. Julep hopped on her bike and coasted down the gravel path.

Huh.

Maybe there was something to this acting thing, after all.